THE COLDEST SAVAGE STOLE MY HEART 2

J. DOMINIQUE

Cole Hart

The Coldest Savage Stole My Heart 2

Copyright © 2019 by J. Dominique

All rights reserved.

Published in the United States of America.

Published by Cole Hart Signature, LLC.

Mailing List

To stay up to date on new releases, plus get information on contests, sneak peeks, and more,

Go To The Website Below...

WWW.COLEHARTSIGNATURE.COM

CHAPTER 1

Nivea

To say I was shocked to see Quad at my door was an understatement. He was definitely the last person I was expecting. I looked him up and down, taking note of the fresh Jordan's and brand new clothes he had on and wondered what in the fuck was really going on here.

"Quad??? What, what the fuck you doin here? Wait…. how are you here?" I stressed with wide eyes. The last time I'd taken the kids to see him, he hadn't said shit about an early release and that wasn't even a month ago.

"Damn, you don't look happy to see a nigga. You gone invite me in at least?" he asked with that same slick ass grin on his face.

"No, come in, come in." I sniffled and tried to wipe my face discreetly as I moved aside so that he could enter. He swaggered past us, taking in my apartment while me and Niyah shared a look. Shit, I was half expecting somebody to pop out and tell me this was some type of joke.

"Girrrrl, what in the whole fuck?" she mumbled under her breath. I shrugged my shoulders cause I was just as

---

J. DOMINIQUE

confused as her ass and tried to steady my pounding heart, before following him into the living room. When I got there, he was standing in front of the couch looking at all of the pictures I had up of the kids.

"Are you gone tell me how the hell you're standing in my apartment Quad?" My voice brought his attention to me, and he looked at me curiously for a second before speaking.

"What I'm not welcome or somethin? That nigga Ju really got you not fuckin with me like that?" He frowned, and I realized he was avoiding the question. He was so good at the shit that I barely even noticed. The fact that he had brought up Judah immediately had me on the defensive and I felt the need to take up for him.

"You know it's not like that, and Judah doesn't have me acting any kind of way. He's fine with us talkin, but I'm just tryin to figure out how you got out when you still have 7 years left on your sentence?" I cocked my head to the side and raised my brows questioningly.

"Right," Niyah cosigned from behind me, causing Quad's gaze to flicker her way.

"That's not important. What is important though is how you had this nigga around my kids and he killed their family! My family!" His voice rose angrily as he peered down at me.

"He wouldn't do no shit like that Quad! Just because the police think he did don't mean shit." Again, I was taking up for Judah, despite my earlier reservations about his involvement. I mean, I slept with this man almost every night. I knew him inside and out; there was no way he had done that shit.

"Ohh, you don't know *Judah* as well as you think you do Niv," he scoffed. "That nigga don't be flexin when he rap! He really bout this street shit! You so damn stupid sometimes, I swear! Did you really think he wanted to be with you and raise some fuckin kids? Huh? Think Niv, what would a 21

2

THE COLDEST SAVAGE STOLE MY HEART 2

year old rapper want with a woman that's 29 with 3 kids?" he questioned, pointing a finger in my face.

"Hey, you need to chill with all that. You ain't gotta be callin her out her name or puttin yo hands on her!" Niyah appeared at my side and said.

"You probly the thot ass bitch that encouraged her to fuck with him in the first place! I see both y'all asses dumb! This nigga start talkin to Nivea and then boom, all of a sudden, my mama and brother dead! You probably led him straight to they ass!" he fumed, narrowing his eyes at us. I flinched away from him and closer to Niyah, who seemed much more brave and confident in Judah's innocence right then. It would have made sense for him to have killed them. Jay was known for doing dumb shit; it would have been just like him to have shot Troy. The question was would Judah have used me to get to Jay?

"You probably had him sleeping here with my kids in the house and shit!" he continued to rant. "What if he hadn't just been satisfied with Jay and my mama. Huh? What if he would have hurt the kids cause you let him in?" He crashed a lamp to the floor, and I shrieked. I had seen Quad angry before but never at me. He was stomping across my floor like he wanted it to cave in and yelling with spit flying from his mouth.

"Oh, hell naw! I ain't gone be disrespected too many more times before I mace yo crazy ass!" Niyah said angrily, grabbing her keys up that held her mace.

"You ain't gone do shit bitch! Got my baby mama out here risking her and my kids' lives!"

"Nigga please! You got yo nerve! The hood talk my nigga and she been riskin her life fuckin with yo clown ass!"

I looked from Niyah to Quad, wondering what she was talking about as they stared each other down. Whatever it was must have been something else he didn't want to talk

3

about because he didn't say shit about it. He just curled his lip in disgust.

"Man, Nivea, get this groupie bitch up outta here! Aghhhh!"

Niyah had maced him as soon as the words left his mouth. He covered his eyes with one hand and held the other one out defensively, as she stood there smirking.

"I told yo stupid ass! Nigga, I ain't Nivea. I'll fuck you up!" she said, attempting to walk up on him, but I stopped her.

"Niyah, what the hell!"

"Don't Niyah me! He ain't been here 5 minutes and he tearin yo shit up and talkin out the side of his face! He only do this shit cause you allow it Nivea! Bet he wouldn't be so tough if Ju was here!" she continued to scream as I held her back.

"Fuck Ju! And fuck you too, bitch!" Quad yelled back.

"Boy I got plenty more mace where that came from, keep playin!"

This shit was too much. In less than two hours, my boyfriend had gotten arrested, my baby daddy who was in jail last time I checked had popped up, and I was breaking up a fight in my living room. It was safe to say that today was not my day.

"Nivea, man, get this nutty bitch outta here so we can talk!" Quad seemed to be recovering from the shot of mace, but he made sure to keep his distance.

"I ain't goin nowhere nigga! You leave!" she snapped, still wrestling against me.

"Niyah, let me just talk to him and I'll call you tomorrow," I told her warily. I knew that I could probably keep Quad in line for the most part; he probably just wanted to vent and, honestly, I still wanted to know how he had gotten out. Niyah, on the other hand, was way too out of control for me right now and I only had the energy to deal with one problem at a time. She looked at me with her mouth dropped open.

"Really Nivea? You puttin me out for him?" She pointed his way with a scowl.

"I just want to get to the bottom of what's goin on Niyah, that's it. I just can't do it with y'all goin back and forth," I tried to explain, but she held her hand up to stop me.

"Nah, it's cool. I need to go check on Troy and find out what's goin on with yo man anyway," she sighed. "Just don't let him be in here doin too much Nivea. I don't trust his ass." She lowered her voice to almost a whisper and looked his way with slanted eyes. I elected not to respond to that directly. She knew exactly what she was doing bringing up Judah.

"Okay, just call me or... I'll call you," I said, thinking better of it. My buzzer went off interrupting whatever it was she was going to say and I let out an aggravated moan. I didn't even want to think about who that could be.

"I'll let whoever that is know you're busy. Be careful," she warned, glaring at Quad one last time before heading to the door. Once I heard it shut behind her, I turned to Quad, hoping I'd get my answers now.

CHAPTER 2

*S*aniyah

You gotta know I was pissed all the way off. Not only was Nivea questioning Ju, but she was up there listening to her snitch ass baby daddy. He was lucky all I'd done was mace him, considering how reckless he was being with them loose ass lips of his. I made sure to slam the door on my way out, so Nivea knew I was mad. I proceeded to take the stairs two at a time until I was at the glass front door. My stomach fluttered a little seeing that Troy was standing on the other side in all his chocolate goodness.

"Where you goin?" he wanted to know, as soon as I pulled the door open. The smell of his cologne invaded my nostrils as he stepped inside, wedging me between him and the door. I almost lost my train of thought standing there with his chest pressed up against mine, but it only took me a second to remember why I was leaving in the first place.

I rolled my eyes towards the stairs and muttered, "I'm goin home, Nivea trippin." He followed my gaze and then looked back at me with his brows knitted over his pretty brown eyes.

"What you mean she trippin? We gotta go get Ju, and you comin home with me," he stated firmly like I didn't have a choice. Instead of arguing with him, I ignored it because honestly, I did want to go home with him. That was if he was still in a good mood after I told him about Quad.

"Quad got out, I don't think she's bouta go nowhere," I said, smacking my lips. The way his eyes darkened when I said that had me a little scared. I drew back a bit, but I was flush up against the door so I didn't get anywhere.

"Fuck he doin over here? She tryna play my boy!" he growled, trying to move past me. I reached out to stop him but was only able to grab ahold of his shirt.

"No! He just showed up out of nowhere! She ain't even know he was gettin out!" I might have been mad at her for entertaining Quad's bullshit, but I wasn't about to let him act like she was on some sneaky shit. He turned his dark eyes on me and then looked down at my hands on him, prompting me to let go. Before I could say anything else, he was on his way up the stairs. I hurried to follow behind him because despite me feeling him, I wasn't about to let him get buck with Nivea. Before I could even reach the landing, I heard him banging on the door loudly with the butt of his gun. I got to him before anybody answered and quietly tried to plead Nivea's case.

"Troy, don't go up in there actin crazy with her. She ain't switchin up on Ju at all, you know she been ridin for him," I reasoned, but he wasn't listening to shit I was saying; he just continued to bang on the door. One of Nivea's neighbors stuck their head out into the hallway, which I knew was a big mistake.

"She's not the only person who lives in this building; keep that shit down before I call the police!" the older woman fussed, giving me and Troy the death stare. He didn't pay her ass any mind either as he banged on the door

7

again. "Did you hear what the fuck I said! I'm calling the cops!"

"Bitch, do I look like I give a fuck!" Troy barked, finally acknowledging the woman who grabbed her chest in shock and gasped loudly. I said a silent prayer that she would realize this nigga was crazy and take her ass back inside. God must have heard me because she slammed her door angrily and Troy continued to knock.

"Who the fuck knockin on my shit like tha-" Quad snapped, swinging the door open but was immediately cut off by Troy's gun going across his shit.

"Oh, my God! Troy stop!" Nivea screamed, coming around the corner. It was like he didn't even hear her as he continued his assault on Quad. She rushed over and tried to push him off, but Troy pinned her with an evil glare that made her back up immediately.

"Stay the fuck back Nivea!" he barked and pointed his gun in Quad's bloody face. "I know exactly what you did hoe ass nigga. Enjoy yo' freedom while you can." He let him go and his body fell limply against the hardwood floor.

"Troy, come on, let's go," I urged, trying to pull him away as he stood over Quad, breathing heavily. By now Nivea, who had been crying hysterically , moved from her spot against the wall and got down on the floor with Quad.

"You foul Nivea," he accused, shaking his head at her before walking away. She watched his retreating back until he disappeared down the stairs, and then she turned her weary eyes on me.

"Just go Niyah." She sighed as her silent tears landed on Quad's face.

"Are you serious? This nigga was just in here talkin to you like you wasn't shit and callin you stupid. Not to mention, he still ain't tell you how he got out did he?" I asked her, curling my lip in irritation. It was crazy how fast she had let him come in and change shit in a half hour. I wanted to blame it on the fact that she was stressed out because she'd just witnessed Ju get arrested for the murder of her kids' people, but I knew it wasn't that. It was like as soon as she saw that there was still a chance for her and Quad, she made up her mind about Ju's guilt.

When she didn't say anything, I blew out a frustrated breath and just walked away from her dizzy ass before I said something I couldn't take back. By the time I made it down the stairs, Troy was pacing back and forth on the phone in front of the building like he hadn't just beat a nigga half to death.

"What the fuck you mean he don't got a bond!" he fumed angrily. I sat listening to one side of the conversation and gathered that he was talking to their lawyer, and there was no way that Ju was getting out, at least not tonight anyway. I still asked anyway, just to be sure.

"What they say?"

"He ain't fuckin getting out! I should go up there and kill that nigga!" He started back in the direction of the building, but I stopped him.

"No! Yo ass gone be in jail next Troy and, besides, you not even A1 yet," I said, placing my hand gently on his chest where he'd gotten shot. He looked like it was taking everything in him not to go back upstairs and finish Quad off.

"Mannn, come on shorty," he grumbled, walking off in the direction of the town car he was riding in. I silently thanked God for him letting it go for now and got in right behind him.

He directed the driver to take us to the Presidential Towers with a heavy sigh, then leaned forward with his elbows on his knees and his head in his hands. I knew he was pissed about the fact that Quad had pulled this bullshit and had sucked Nivea in. Real shit, I was mad about the shit too. After riding in silence for a few minutes, he looked over at me in the dark car and murmured, "Come here Niyah."

I slowly scooted closer to him until I was right by his side, but he pulled me into his lap, instead, and wrapped his arms around my waist.

Even though it hadn't been that long since I'd met Troy, the chemistry was off the chain between us. He was laid back and funny, just like I liked them. Since he had gotten released from the hospital, we had kicked it a couple of times and it was always good vibes when I was in his presence. Tonight was supposed to have been chill, just like any other night we were together, but Ju getting locked up and Nivea acting crazy had fucked it all up.

"I'm mad as fuck I can't light that goofy nigga up!" He frowned, clenching his fists.

"Don't be, he's gone get his for this shit," I told him, running my hand over his waves. "I shoulda tased his ass instead of just macing him."

"You maced him?" he asked, trying to hide the grin that was appearing on his face.

"Hell yeah! His mouth too reckless for me." I shrugged. Nivea might have put up with that shit, but I wasn't. His grin widened in the dark car and he pulled me closer.

"My lil gangsta," he mused, looking up at me with hooded eyes while he rubbed my thighs and butt softly. The shit was feeling so good; I didn't even resist him when he leaned up to kiss me with those soft ass lips. He was giving me short juicy kisses at first, but it quickly deepened as he sucked my bottom lip into his mouth. I felt him harden beneath me and my heart raced at how big he was. It didn't take long for him to find his way inside of the romper I was wearing, and I shuddered as his fingers brushed across my clit.

"Damn Niyah, you wet as fuck," he noted in my ear as he dipped a finger inside of me and rubbed my wetness against my nub. My mouth fell open, and I moaned softly from the pleasure he was inflicting on me. I never knew I'd be so turned on from a nigga with his tongue in my ear and his finger in my pussy in the back of a town car. I held on to him tightly as I grinded against his thumb, and he whispered all types of nasty shit in my ear.

"Fuuuuuck, I can't wait to dig up in this wet ass pussy Niyah; get this lil nut up out the way, so we can go upstairs. I'm tryna taste you, baby."

Now, why he have to say that? My ears felt like they were going to pop and my stomach tightened, letting me know I was close to coming. Besides the sound of Troy growling that freaky shit, all that could be heard was a sound like macaroni being stirred.

"Ummmm Troy, shit!" I screeched, quivering as I came and my clit pulsed. I was stuck for a minute and, when I finally got myself together and opened my eyes, we were in front of his building. I hadn't even realized the car had stopped. Embarrassment flooded me and I cocked my head, covering my mouth. "Oh, my God, how long we been here?"

Troy, who was completely unbothered, removed his hand from my shorts and licked his fingers with a shrug. "Shit, like 5 minutes. You straight though shorty, let's go." He gave a light tap on the window and the driver opened up the door and reached a hand out to help me. I was sure my face was a special shade of red as I let him help me out of the car and onto the sidewalk, where Troy met me with a grin. My shorts were wet and sticking to the inside of my thigh and I could see that Troy had a wet spot as well. He put his arms around my waist once he reached me and lifted my chin so that I was looking up into his handsome face.

"I'm not goin in there like this nigga," I said, adamantly

shaking my head. This place looked like it was crawling with uptight ass white people and I was not in the mood to be stared at.

"Girl, these people in here ain't worried bout you; it's late as fuck. Ain't nobody down here but Jeffrey the doorman." He laughed and grabbed ahold of my hand. "Now, come on, I'm tryna go swimmin." The look he gave me let me know that he wasn't talking about swimming in their complimentary pool, and it had my pussy ready. So, instead of putting up a fuss, I let him lead me inside of the grand lobby, which was empty besides the black concierge that sat behind the desk. He frowned when he saw Troy and me walking through but didn't say anything as we made our way to the elevators. "Sup Jeffrey!" Troy called out when he noticed him looking our way. His frown deepened and he returned to whatever it was he was doing behind the desk.

"He ain't look happy to see you," I chuckled, stepping onto the elevator behind Troy.

"That's cuz his name ain't Jeffrey." He shrugged with a smirk and pressed the button for the sixth floor. "But his ass look just like the nigga off Fresh Prince, don't he?" We both busted up laughing because he definitely did look like the butler from that show. I shook my head at his silly ass, glad that he was in a lighter mood than he was an hour before. Ju being locked up for murder had been a blow to all of us, but I knew that he was taking it harder than anybody else. He leaned against the back wall and grabbed the thin fabric of my romper, pulling me into him.

"I'm sorry about Ju," I murmured quietly as I gazed up into his eyes. His jaw tightened and his body went stiff, letting me know that he his light mood was gone.

"He ain't gone be there long, but you bouta take my mind off it anyway," he said, kissing me so deep that my knees buckled just as the doors dinged open. I nodded when we finally separated, unable to speak right away. He gave me a panty-dropping smile and locked his fingers with mine, leading me into the hallway and to his apartment door. I was more than ready to take his mind off of anything that he wanted me to and I planned to do just that.

CHAPTER 3

Savage

"Your honor, my client has no criminal record and is only here because of false allegations. The police have no physical evidence. I ask that he be released on bond, immediately." My lawyer, Dean, addressed the judge who looked down at us over the rims of his glasses. I was trying to keep my anger in check for even having to go through this shit right now, but it was hard. I hadn't ever been to jail, simply because I was careful and smart about everything that I did. That's one of the main reasons I was so pissed.

I'd slacked and let that nigga Keys live way longer than he should have and, now, I was in jail because of it. I glanced back to see my OG, lil sister, Troy Pree, and Mone sitting directly behind me. Although I still wasn't fucking with them, I was glad that they had come to show their support. I searched the crowded court room for Nivea and, when I didn't see her, I gave Troy a questioning look. He shrugged and shook his head, telling me he didn't know where she was. Disappointment filled me, but I kept it cool. There was probably a good reason why she wasn't here with everybody else. I refused to believe that she wasn't fucking with me off the word of the police.

"We'd like to request that bond be denied your honor," the bitch ass state attorney spoke, interrupting my thoughts. He looked at me with a smug expression. "The defendant may not have any priors, but that just means that he's good at criminal activity. I believe that he would be a flight risk-."

"Objection! He's speculating. There is no evidence that my client would be a flight risk," Dean scoffed. "On the contrary, he has obligations that prevent him from leaving the city, let alone the state."

"Both of you need to save it for the trial. We are merely here to find out the defendant's plea," the judge said, banging his gavel.

"Not guilty your honor," Dean answered.

"Well, due to the fact that the defendant doesn't have any prior record, I'm going to set bond at $100,000. We are adjourned."

I breathed a sigh of relief as my lawyer patted me on the back, and my O.G. shouted, "Thank God!" I wanted to tell them to unshackle me right now, but I still had property at the jail and I needed to get my shit.

"Aye, we bouta get that right now and I'ma be on my way to come get you," Troy let me know and gave me a dap. The shorty Niyah was at his side now. She looked happy to know I was getting out, but her girl still wasn't here. My lawyer ushered me out as they called the next case. I was more than ready to get up out of there. Them days behind bars away from Nivea and the kids was hard, not because I couldn't handle it, but because I had been around them damn near every day for months. Having to sit in a cell and wake up without QJ's knee in my side or Quiana singing at the top of her lungs and asking a million questions, without Kymia complaining or Nivea's smile was the tough part. I'd grown accustomed to them; they were my family now, and I was ready to get back to them.

Walking out the doors of the jail, I spotted Troy's cocaine white Audi right away. He stood posted up against it with his arms folded, and I shook my head at his ass. This nigga was already spending money on big shit, and we hadn't even earned it yet. His face split into a wide grin once he saw me coming towards him. "My nigga," he said, shaking my hand and pulling me into a hug.

"I see you out here shining." I nodded towards the car and his grin grew even wider as he admired it with me.

"Yeah, I had to make sure you was riding clean when you left this bitch, so I pulled out the newest member in the fleet."

"That's what's up, but where the bud at?" I questioned. "I'm tryna get my mind right before I go see Nivea." He gave me an uncomfortable expression and scratched the back of his head.

"Right, right. Let's ride." I could already tell that what he was about to say was gone piss me off. I had a feeling that Nivea wasn't fucking with me like that, and I guess I could understand considering the fact that these were her kids' people that I was accused of killing. Still though, she had been up under a nigga for months, the least she could do was hear me out.

As soon as we got inside the car, Troy handed me the blunt and a lighter, before cutting up his radio and pulling off. I decided not to say anything right away, hoping that the effects of some grade A weed would put me in a relaxed state. We rode for a while smoking, and then he lit another one before he finally opened his mouth.

"What I'm bouta tell you is fucked up my G, but it really ain't no way to sugar coat it," he said, looking from me to the midday traffic.

"Then, just gone head spit it out man, you talkin like I'ma

16

bitch or somethin." I frowned. He handed me the new blunt he'd lit up and ran a hand down his face.

"Man, Nivea baby daddy out." He sighed and gave me a cryptic look, causing me to choke on the smoke I'd been holding in my lungs. There was no way I had heard this nigga right. He couldn't have been talking about Quad's bitch ass. What fucking bargaining chip could he use to get out, when nobody fucked with him? My mind raced, wondering if that nigga had snitched on me to get out and how he even knew to tell anybody.

"Fuck you mean *he out?*" I questioned, even though I knew exactly what he meant. Keys had talked all that shit about him and then ran straight to dude's snitch ass and put a bug in his ear.

"That nigga *out*," Troy stressed the word and bucked his eyes at me, "and he at Nivea's." He flinched as he told me, knowing that I was about to blow up.

"Take me over there." My voice was cool, not giving away how agitated I truly was, but Troy already knew me. So, he knew what was up as soon as I said that.

"You out on bond nigga! You gotta stay out the way and you know if you go over there, it's gone fuck up any chance we have at correctin shit," he warned.

"Do I look like I give a fuck! I was locked up 3 days and shorty already back with that rat ass nigga!"

"You over there worried about the wrong shit. I can't lie; I fuck with Nivea, but she should be the least of yo concerns right now! Take care of this case first, then get at yo girl," he reasoned, making a lot of sense. The bigger issue wasn't that Quad had gotten Nivea to take him back, it was that the nigga was still breathing.

"You right," I agreed verbally, even though inside I was already planning to drive over to her house as soon as he dropped me off. It would probably be the worst torture to see Nivea with him, but I had to see it for myself. Troy wouldn't understand that; hell, three months ago, I wouldn't have understood either.

"Hell naw, you said that shit way too fast, you ain't slick." He shook his head and sighed. "I can already tell you thinkin bout pullin up on her... you know what, fuck it. I might as well just take you over there, least I know you won't do nothin stupid with me around."

That's what his ass think? I said to myself but, to him, I said, "I just need to see this shit for myself man; I ain't tryna do nothin to her or him." I could feel him giving me a crazy ass look, but I kept my eyes on the street ahead of us. He hit a few blocks to get us to her house, since we had been heading in the opposite direction to mine. Pulling up in front of her building, it was dead outside besides a few kids playing here and there on the block. I could see her car parked right across the street from her door, but she wasn't in it. I wasn't sure what I was expecting to see, just on some pullup shit. It wasn't like I would be able to see in her windows or no shit like that anyway. It took me all of two minutes to realize that and, just as I was about to tell Troy to pull off, the door to her building opened and out she walked. At the sight of her, my chest got tight. The anger I thought I was going to feel was nonexistent when I finally laid eyes on her. I assumed that this was what Pree had been talking about that night in the car. Nivea had my ass wide open, sitting outside her crib on some old Jodeci shit.

My mood changed quick as fuck though when Quad stepped out behind her. I gritted my teeth together as I watched him walk up on her, and whatever he was saying put a smile on her face. Instinctively, my hand went for my gun while I pulled at the door handle but Troy stopped me, grabbing ahold of my shoulder.

"Nigga, what the fuck is you doin!" he questioned,

looking at me like I'd lost my mind and, in a way, I had. If nothing else, I at least half expected shorty to be as tore up as I had been, but she was all in her glow and Quad was right there looking like he was ready to suck the Dove soap suds out her ass. I didn't even respond as I snatched away and continued towards the couple, knowing that he was right behind me, regardless of whether or not I was wrong for what I was about to do.

By the time I made it across the street, they were both inside of the silver, 2018 Lexus truck I'd gifted her not too long ago, with him on the driver's side. This infuriated me and had me closing the small distance between me and them like I grew wings.

"What the fuck!" Quad tried to sound tough but piped all the way down when I reached across Nivea and put my gun in his face.

"Oh, my God, Judah! What the hell are you doin?" Nivea shrieked fearfully. I never took my eyes off her bitch ass baby daddy though, as my mouth twisted into a sinister smirk. If for no other reason than him being with my woman, in my car, about to go get my kids, I wanted to send a bullet through his head, and that let me further know how deep I had fallen.

Troy reached the driver's side door then and pulled it open, drawing Quad's attention away briefly as I tucked my gun and finally acknowledged Nivea. "Come holla at me," I gritted, moving away to allow her room. A small bit of irritation hit me when she shook her head no, leaning further back in her seat like I wouldn't pull her ass out.

"You ain't gotta do shit Niv-!" Quad chimed before Troy cracked him across his shit, causing him to yelp in pain.

"Shut yo bitch ass up nigga!" Troy hissed.

I silently eyed Nivea with my eyebrows raised; it only took her a second to realize that I wasn't asking her and she quickly undid her seat belt and stepped out of the car to stand in front of me.

"This what the fuck you doin shorty, you couldn't even give me a chance to talk to you before you ran back to this goofy muthafucka right here?" I pointed to Quad without taking my eyes off of her. Even though I hadn't raised my voice, my anger was evident and so was her fear; she had her body pressed into the side of the truck like she was scared I might do something to HER. The same nigga that she had been laying up with, the same nigga that had taken her kids to numerous places, with AND without her. I wanted to tell her that if I'd wanted them dead, I could have done that with ease but, considering the current situation, saying so probably wouldn't help my case.

"Judah," she said calmly with her hands raised to keep distance between us.

"Don't talk to me like that Niv, you know damn well I wouldn't hurt you." I took a single step closer, planting one hand around her waist and cupping her face with the other. Her body went tense at me touching her and she narrowed her eyes.

"Do I know that? You don't have to pretend anymore, okay! Your mission is complete, right?" she scoffed, folding her arms over her chest, her fear suddenly gone.

"Yo, you bugged the fuck out Niv! You let this nigga who don't even know me come fill yo head with bullshit instead of waitin to talk to me! You, of all people, know I don't do shit I don't want to do! If I was really just usin you, I coulda been dipped! Fuck I'm spendin time with lil man for? Huh? Why I'm makin promises to Ms. Q and Ky then?!"

"I really don't know but-,"

"Yo ass know exactly why Niv! I been here and where the fuck this bitch ass nigga been?!" I pointed towards the car, where Quad sat silently with his face balled up at the ill shit I said about him.

"I'm not tryna do this right now," she argued while shaking her head as she tried to move away from me, but I snatched her ass back to me.

"When we gone do it then, huh? You lettin this nigga and the police get in yo head without even talkin to me! You ready to turn yo back on me that fast?" Shorty had me out here emotional as hell. I had invested time and energy into her and her kids; how was I supposed to function, let alone handle what I needed to knowing that part of my problem was sleeping in my fucking bed at night?

"Well, here's your chance Judah, did you?" she questioned, tilting her head to the side. "Did you kill my kids' family?"

I let out a deep breath and looked away, unable to meet the hard stare she was giving me. The truth was even if I wanted to be completely honest, I couldn't and wouldn't ever implicate myself. Not even to Nivea. I couldn't trust her with the truth of things, but I couldn't necessarily deny some shit I'd done either. Electing to remain quiet, I just shook my head and stepped away from her with a scowl.

"It wouldn't matter anyway now, would it? Yo ass done already showed me who you ridin with," my voice came out dejectedly. I couldn't even front, Nivea had me sick as hell.

"No Judah, don't try and turn this shit on me! You don't get to do that!" she yelled, but I was already walking off on her goofy ass. I was done with the conversation and done with her too, until I snatched away her baby daddy's last breath. By the time Troy and I climbed back in the car, Quad had finally gotten his bitch ass out and they stood arguing in the street, but I told Troy to keep going.

"You straight man?" he asked after a few minutes.

"Shit, I will be."

"Listen, that shit was fucked up. I really wanted to go

across that nigga shit again, but let's keep you outta jail first, then we can worry about Nivea," he suggested, probably realizing that I was anything but straight. What he said was right though. I needed to focus on my freedom and then I could work on the cuffs Niv had on my damn heart.

"You right. I'm good bro, just take me out to Olympia Fields." I wasn't looking at him, but I could feel his eyes on me.

"Nigga, who the fuck you know out that way?"

"I do," I told him, punching in the address on his navigation system. "I was gone surprise Niv and the kids with it after the party." I shrugged and brought my attention back to the streets whipping by.

"Damnnnnn," Troy dragged, letting out a low whistle.

"Yeah, I know, right."

Unable to find the words to try and lessen the multiple blows I'd just gotten, Troy didn't say shit else. But, what could he say? I had went against my own relationship plans and basically got played. A nigga was sick but, still, I couldn't see myself letting her go.

By the time we were finally pulling into the circular driveway, I was more than ready to lie down, hoping that after a good night's rest, I would be up and ready to take care of anything standing in the way of my freedom.

"Damn nigga, this shit big as hell, and you got a fuckin fountain in yo front yard!" Troy noted, gazing up at the house through the windshield.

"Hell yeah, this shit nice man," I told him and a hint of sadness touched my voice.

"Look man, shit gone work out for y'all and, if it don't, we can turn this bitch to a playboy mansion on some real shit. Just get some rest and hit me up tomorrow, so we can start puttin shit in motion," he finally said, realizing that I wasn't in a joking mood.

"Bet."

I stepped out of the car and trudged to the front door to let myself in, further reminded of the house's emptiness by the way my footsteps echoed as soon as I stepped in the foyer. The only room I had placed any furniture in was me and Niv's. I'd planned on bringing her there the night of the party to show her that I'd bought us a home as my first big purchase. I was gone fuck shorty ass all over this big mutha fucka, but shit ain't work out like that and now I was sitting in this big bitch alone. One thing was for damn certain though, I wasn't gone be alone for long. Whether Nivea knew it or not, her and the kids was gone be coming there soon, and I put that on Quad's head.

CHAPTER 4

*N*ivea

    I hadn't expected for Judah to be out of jail that fast, and I damn sure hadn't thought that he would come over to my house but, then again, I should have known he would come for me. Looking into his face almost had me forgetting what type of a monster he was; my love for him momentarily made my heart start beating faster, ready to jump into his arms. It didn't take him long though to remind me of the reason why I'd decided to leave him alone in the first place. Despite the love I could see in his eyes, his face showed just how angry he was. I guess I could understand why, but what did he expect from me? He had USED ME, had used my need for love to get close to the people my children called family. He'd been lying in all of our faces for months, and he'd even helped to comfort them a few times, not that they were truly torn up about it. Kymia was very nonchalant about the whole thing, but Quiana and QJ were both too young to understand. Still, I couldn't just overlook the fact that he had done something like that and carried on like everything was okay.

"I can't believe yo stupid ass had that nigga around my fuckin kids man!" Quad fussed from the passenger seat. "Do you see what the fuck I was talkin bout?! He was ready to kill both our asses!" I couldn't help the snort that escaped my lips at how loud he was trying to get with me.

"If he was gone kill us, he would have done it, but I doubt highly if it was gone be me that he did somethin to," I mumbled the last part but, from the way his head whipped around, I knew that he had heard me.

"Oh, you think his ass woulda spared you?" he chuckled like he knew something I didn't and shook his head. "He don't discriminate! Yo ass woulda been laid out here right next to me! He don't give a fuck about you, not more than his freedom anyway. I told you not to get out the truck, but you was so pressed to be in that nigga face!" Now, it was my turn to look at him crazy. Quad was acting like I willingly got out to talk to him, instead of being forced out by his mean ass.

"No, you told me and I quote, *you ain't gotta do shit Nivea!*" I mimicked and smacked my lips. "It ain't like yo ass was gone do shit if he snatched me outta here!" I was getting so damn tired of his mouth. He'd been talking shit the whole damn weekend about me and Judah and, I could admit that it was mostly my guilt that had allowed him to speak freely, but I wasn't gone be too many more stupid asses. Being with Judah had given me a low tolerance for excepting just anything from people and, despite his faults, I appreciated that.

"Are you crazy! They had a fuckin gun in my face! What the fuck was I sposed to do?" he fumed angrily.

"You was sposed to do exactly what you did." I rolled my eyes and sighed heavily. "Nothin."

"Let me stop talkin before I have to smack the shit out yo silly ass!"

"Yeah, that's yo best bet cause the day you slap me is the

day yo ass gone meet yo heavenly father." I could feel his eyes on me burning a hole in the side of my face, but I ignored his whining ass. The last thing I was worried about was him laying a finger on me. If he hadn't already noticed, he soon would, that I wasn't the same Nivea that I used to be.

"So, you tough now?" he questioned, mugging me.

"Hell, *you tough now?*" I heard him grumble under his breath and knew that he had called me a bitch. I decided to let it go because he had already just had a near death experience and I didn't want to pick up my kids with an attitude. They'd already probably be confused as hell about the fact that their father was out.

We spent the remainder of the ride over to my mother's in silence, with him huffing and puffing like a bitch and me ignoring him. Despite what I now knew that he'd done, Judah was heavy on my mind. A bitch was feeling real life guilty because even though Judah hadn't denied killing them, my heart still pulled off in that car with him. Honestly, I didn't even need him to admit it, and that was the worst part.

Quad had finally broke down and told me about getting a letter from his brother's friend implicating Judah and how he'd turned it over as evidence to get a reduced sentence. He said that he didn't really want to admit it to me, let alone Niyah because he ain't want to be labeled a snitch. I thought that was an odd ass reason, considering that he didn't owe anybody his loyalty besides his family, but I figured it was a street dude thing and I let it go. That letter had been the nail in the coffin for Judah to me and that was why I'd been willing to leave him alone, but that wasn't so easy with him in my face. I had damn near melted when he held me in his arms, which was why I had to sober myself up by asking him about the murders. Even though he didn't answer me, the hardest part of that whole confrontation was him walking away from me.

I ended up pulling into my mama's driveway not even an hour later and prepared myself to face my kids and the million and one questions that I knew they would ask. They must have been waiting for me because Quiana and Kymia were outside before I could even make it around the truck. From the looks on their faces, I could tell that they had heard about Judah, but what I wasn't expecting was for them to be worried about him.

"Ma, is Ju out?"

"Why the police tryna say he did it?"

"Can we go see him if he not out?"

They bombarded me with question after question, both looking frustrated over the situation, but not for the reason I would have thought. I willed myself not to shed any tears at the fact that my kids were ready to side with Judah over everybody, no questions asked, and it hadn't taken much to convince me of his guilt. They were kids though and kid's mostly saw things from a certain point of view, but I wasn't about to kill their hopes just yet.

"Uhhh Judah... he ummm," I stuttered, unable to bring myself to lie to them. I was so distracted trying to come up with an excuse that I didn't notice Quad get out of the car and come stand beside me.

"Now, why y'all askin bout that nigga when I came all this way to see y'all?" he asked with a wide grin on his face.

"Daddy!!!!" Quiana shouted, jumping into his outstretched arms while the cool queen Kymia stood back, taking him in. I instantly breathed a sigh of relief since they were distracted for the moment.

"Dang Ky, you ain't gone show me some love?" Quad finally noticed that she hadn't ran over and asked, reaching an arm out for her. For a second, she looked hesitant to get any closer to him but, eventually, she trudged his way and gave him a stiff one-arm hug with her face blank, not giving off any emotion.

"How'd you get out?" her voice was dry as hell and I wondered if he was picking up the vibe that she wasn't happy to see him. He must not have because he gave her arm a squeeze and shrugged.

"They let me out today for good behavior." Her silence caused him to peer my way, unaware of the ill feelings that she had towards him. Thankfully, Nadia walked her ratchet ass outside dressed in some white jeans that were ripped on the knees and a royal blue, off the shoulder sweater. When she saw Quad, her eyes got big as hell and she glanced my way with a sneaky smirk before addressing him.

"Dammmmn, they finally let the real out I see," she observed, giving Quad a hug. He released Kymia so that he could wrap an arm around Nadia, and she used that opportunity to run inside.

"You know they can't keep a nigga down." Quad chuckled and so did she.

"So, does this mean you and Niv are back together?" she asked, looking between the both of us.

"Hell yeah! We back like I never left," he told her before I could get a word out. I narrowed my eyes at him in irritation because I had told him when he first popped his ass back up on my doorstep that it wasn't like that. He thought that shit was cute, but I didn't find it funny at all.

"Okayyyy, I know that's right!" Nadia hyped his ass up and I rolled my eyes.

"I'm bouta go grab QJ," I grumbled, not talking to anybody in particular; I just honestly wanted to get away from both their dumbasses.

They continued to make small talk as I made my way inside, calling out for my mama as soon as I hit the door.

"Girl, I done told yo ass to stop yellin in here! You wake

this baby up, I'ma beat yo ass!" she chastised from her spot on the couch. QJ laid beside her knocked out, with drool spilling out his mouth. I took a seat across from her and sat my purse down next to me.

"Sorry, ma," I barely got out before Quad, Quiana and Nadia filed into the house.

"Grandma, my daddy here!" Quiana happily shouted, dragging him in by the arm. I didn't miss the look of distaste that my mama had upon seeing Quad.

"Hello Quadeem."

"Hey, Ms. Hynes, how you doin?" he asked, letting Quiana pull him into a chair next to my mama, where he pulled out a damn iPhone X and handed it to her. I couldn't help but wonder how in the fuck he had time to get a damn phone when my house was supposedly his first stop once he'd gotten out. He had obviously lied, but I wasn't going to trip about it in front of my mama and sister nosy ass.

"Hmph, I've been better," she replied dryly and then turned her attention my way. "Can you come help me wrap up these plates for the kids Nivea?"

I knew from the look on her face that she wasn't really requesting, so I ignored the small giggle that Nadia was doing and followed my mama into the kitchen. She went around her small island, pulled out five paper plates, and began piling them with the cabbage and corned beef that she had cooked.

"I'm gone assume that he's the reason Kymia just ran her ass up in here lookin crazy," she finally said, never looking up from her task.

"You know she get in her moods mama-"

"She does, but she in a mood now cause she don't like that nigga, and I can't say that I blame her cause I can't stand his ass either," she cut me off, finally meeting my confused gaze. I had known that there was a small rift between her and

Quad, but I thought that it was because of him being in and out of jail. It wasn't like I expected to bring Quad over here and they automatically click, but Ky and my mama both were being dramatic as fuck.

"I'm not about to feed into her bullshit right now ma, I got enough to deal with." I sighed, thinking about the fact that my baby daddy had just gotten out of jail by breaking street code, and my new nigga had betrayed me and my kids by using me to get to someone else.

"Oh, like Judah?" She raised her brows. "Boy probably wasn't in jail a whole twenty-four hours and you already back with your tired ass baby daddy." She shook her head at me with a look of pity on her beautiful face.

"Really ma? From what I could tell, you ain't too much care for Judah either."

"You're right, he's young and wild, but he stepped all the way up and I can't do shit but respect it; plus, he made you happy. Way happier than that no good ass Quad." She frowned, surprising me once again. My mama hadn't flat out said that she didn't like Judah, but she wasn't all super warm to him, so to hear her vouching for him shocked the shit out of me.

"Well, tell me how you really feel ma," I grumbled.

"Ain't that what I just did?"

I was almost sure that was a rhetorical question so I stayed quiet, hoping that there would be an end to this conversation sometime in the next minute or so.

"Anyway," she rolled her eyes, "all I'm saying is that you don't have to feel obligated to be with somebody because of some false sense of loyalty. Don't let Quad come in and steal your happiness from you."

"Judah is being accused of killin Brenda and Jay, ma. How am I supposed to be happy with somebody who killed two innocent people, that happen to be related to my ex and my kids?"

"Girl, I'd hardly call that bitch Brenda innocent, and we all know Jay's no good ass wasn't either but, besides the words of others, what do you got that makes you believe that shit so easily? Don't even answer that cause I already know." She held her hand up to stop the objection I was about to make. "I don't know why you feel like you don't deserve good things, but don't demonize that boy because you're scared to accept something great. God sent him to you and the devil sent Quad. Now, do you wanna go to heaven or hell?" Her face showed that she was dead ass serious, so I choked on the laugh that threatened to escaped. How she thought I was going to hell if I was with Quad was beyond me.

"Nivea, I gotta go do somethin right quick; can you drop me off?" Quad called out, and I can't say that I didn't let out a breath of relief, while my mama looked at me as if her point had just been proven. Finally done with the kids' plate, she pushed them over to me and I counted out four, letting me know that she hadn't made Quad one. I for real didn't even want to argue with her, so I didn't mention it as I picked them up.

"Yeah!" I shouted back before turning back to my mama. "Thanks ma." I lifted the bag of plates and started out of the kitchen, glad to be free of the intense conversation.

When I made it into the living room, Quad was struggling with a whiny QJ, while Nadia sat a little too close to him for my taste. Quiana was no longer in the room, so I was guessing she had gone to get her things together so that we could leave. Frowning, I came over to the two and, as soon as my baby saw me, he started acting worse.

"Man, what the fuck wrong with him Niv!" Quad

snapped, letting him down so that he could run to me and latch on to my leg.

"I don't know, maybe he doesn't recognize you." I shrugged, as Quad gave me a look that could kill before squatting down eye level to him.

"Hey man, you don't know me? I'm yo daddy." He sounded irritated by the fact that his only son wasn't trying to fuck with him but, again, that was his fault. It wasn't much that I could do about that either, but it definitely didn't help that QJ shook his head no and immediately asked for Judah. I prayed that Quad didn't catch on to what he was saying since his speech wasn't perfect, but he must have because the next thing I knew, he was on his feet and breathing all hard into my face.

"Man, what the fuck he callin me dude name for?" I was at a loss for words, and Nadia just sat there laughing like that shit was funny. "See, this is why I ain't want you shackin up with that nigga! Y'all out here playin house with my kids, got them not even fuckin with me!"

"Ut uhh, what you not about to do is be raisin your voice at me. Of course he gone ask about the nigga that been around him every day for months; it ain't his fault or mine that you haven't been around like that. You actin like he called him daddy or somethin!" See, Quad was still used to the quiet pushover me, but that shit was about to be dead. I may have tolerated a lot of shit from him in the past, but Judah had changed all of that. He waved me off, unmoved.

"You might as well!" he got loud again, and I refrained from hauling off and slapping a booger out his ass.

"You know what, I ain't bouta go back and forth with you in my damn mama house. We'll talk bout this later once we get home. Now, can you carry these to the car for me while I finish getting the kids ready?" He looked like he wanted to object but thought better of it. Nadia might have been right there laughing and shit, but my mama already ain't like him, add to that the fact that he was getting loud with her child, in her house. I was surprised she hadn't already come out brandishing a butcher knife.

Even though it was obvious that he didn't want to, Quad just grabbed the plates and I handed him the keys too so that he could stay his ass outside. I was ready to drop him off asap cause the day was turning out to be a disaster. As soon as he closed the door behind him, I sat down to wait on the girls, ignoring the looks I could feel Nadia giving me.

"Leave me alone Dia."

"I ain't even say shit." She scrunched up her forehead.

"You was bout to."

"Girl boom, ain't nobody thinking bout you and Quad, shit; hell, I'm used to y'all arguing." She waved me off, and I hated to admit that she was right. Your man being in jail had a way of making you only remember the good times, and we'd had a lot of those, but we had some fucked up times too and, the longer Quad was around me, I was beginning to be reminded of those bad times.

Right then, Quiana and Kymia came down the stairs both holding their book bags with their changes of clothes, so I decided to drop the conversation. I grabbed Quad Jr.'s little back pack and stood to my feet so that I could go. The girls headed out of the door first, with me and QJ right behind them.

"Mama was right you know," Nadia said, just before I stepped out. I placed half my body back into the doorway and raised my brows in confusion.

"Huh?"

"I said mama was right, you know, the stuff she was just tellin you in the kitchen. You and Ju are weird as fuck together, but I like him way more for you," she said simply and then turned back to the t.v. As bad as I wanted to ask her

33

more, I couldn't because for one, QJ was pulling me out the door and, for two, I was fucked up over the fact that her and Quad had heard our conversation, yet he hadn't said anything and Nadia agreed with her. I left confused and in my own thoughts, with Judah and our situation heavy on my mind. Quad probably was attributing my silence the whole ride as me being angry, but it was more so me being stuck on what I should do. Should I ignore the fact that the nigga I loved killed two people just for my own happiness, or should I go back to my old nigga just because he was now available to me?

Shit.

Decisions. Decisions.

CHAPTER 5

Troy

I tried hitting my nigga Ju phone for what felt like the hundredth time and got the voicemail again. Either the nigga was MIA because he was looking for that fuck nigga Keys, or he was still holed up in that big ass house tripping about Nivea. Considering the situation, I was going with the latter. I felt bad about him going through it on account of me, but he needed to shake that hurt off and get his ass up. Which was exactly why I was on my way out to go and pick his ass up.

"Aye, I'm bouta get up outta here," I told a sleeping Niyah and rubbed her exposed thigh. We had been vibing real heavy since we'd met and I couldn't lie, I fucked with shorty. She was fine as hell, smart and she got her bag by any means. I saw a lot of traits in her that I could relate to and, even though I had really only been planning on a smash and dash, I ended up constantly coming back for more, and it was far beyond the physical.

"Mmmm, I need to get my ass up too," she moaned and stretched her small frame across her bed. That move alone had me ready to take my shit off and lay my ass back down with her. She rolled over onto her back and looked up at me with half closed eyes.

"Damn girl, you fine as hell," came out of my mouth before I could stop it and she threw her head back and laughing like I'd said the funniest joke ever. "I ain't playin, I'm ready to jump back in that muthafucka with you." She sat up and crawled over to where I stood on the side of the bed and put her arms around my neck. Despite a night full of savage ass sex, shorty still smelled sweet as fuck and, on instinct, my mans stood at attention.

"As tempting as that sounds, I gotta go to work and you gotta go help Ju clear his name." She looked at me seriously and, if it was possible, my dick got even harder. Shorty was definitely a keeper.

"Facts, but I'm definitely comin back through here when you get off, or you can come to my spot. I'ma tell Jeffrey to let you up," I told her, palming her plump ass in both of my hands.

"Okay, it might be late though cause I told them I'd do a 12 hour shift tonight." I nodded silently and mumbled an okay, as she planted light kisses on my lips. As hard as it was, I pulled away and put some distance between us so that I could start gathering my shit to go. I didn't miss the pout on shorty's lips as she climbed off the bed and headed to the bathroom to shower. She ain't even realize that if I had kept on sitting there letting her kiss on me, neither one of us was gonna leave. After grabbing my keys and phone from her nightstand, I turned to leave.

"Hey! What's the doorman's *real* name?" she called out with her head poking out of the door. "I just don't wanna be callin him Jeffrey when I get over there." I shrugged and tried to think of anytime I had ever heard that nigga's real name but kept coming up with a blank. I'd never been interested in finding out his real name since, off top, he'd struck me as a Jeffrey.

"Shiiiit, I don't even know; ever since I met that nigga, I been callin him that." She rolled her eyes playfully and smacked her lips.

"Oh, my God! I'll just ask him when I get there," she huffed.

"That's all you had to do anyway," I teased, further irritating her as I left out, ignoring whatever smart ass comment she was saying when I closed the door behind myself.

As soon as I stepped outside, the heat damn near melted my ass and I hurried to get into my truck and cut on the a.c. I decided not to try and call Ju again since his ass had been playing about not answering his phone and just jumped straight on the e-way headed to Olympia Fields with NBA Youngboy blasting.

When I finally pulled into the gate at this nigga's crib, I parked behind his little ass car and stepped out, leaving my shit running. Before I could ring the doorbell, I saw that the door was cracked, and I instantly pulled his gun out and pushed it open the rest of the way. Without making any noise, I walked through each room of that big ass house, coming up empty in every one of them. The only room that looked like it had been lived in was the living room where bottles and weed baggies were scattered all over, even though he had a whole bed upstairs but a ball of blankets laid on the floor underneath the window. I kicked a Wendy's bag out of my way and crossed the room confused as hell.

"The fuck?" I grumbled. "I know this nigga ain't left with nobody."

I headed back out of the house, now irritated that it seemed like I'd wasted a damn trip. My first thought was that maybe his ass had went back to Nivea's; without me there, that could turn into a fucked up situation. I rushed out of the door, making sure to lock up behind myself, ready to peel out and stop his ass from doing something crazy but, as I passed his car, I slowed down. Something was telling me to look inside, and I walked around to the driver's side where Ju was laid out with an empty D'usse bottle in his lap.

"This nigga," I huffed, snatching the door open. "Man Ju, get yo ass up nigga!" I grabbed his ass by the front of his shirt and pulled him out, making the bottle fall from his hand and break on the ground.

"Man, get the fuck up off me." He struggled against the hold I had on him, but he wasn't a match for me considering that he was fucked up. I frowned at how bad this nigga smelled and the clothes that he still had on since I'd dropped him off.

"Yo ass out here trippin' nigga! You gone fuck around and go to jail out here on some ole sucka for love ass shit!" I couldn't believe my mans was out here bad like this. I knew I shouldn't have left his ass by himself the other day. Now, his ass had wasted two whole days getting fucked up and feeling sorry for himself. That shit was just gone give Keys a chance to go off the fucking grid, since the news stations and sleazy ass tabloids had leaked that he was out.

"Get off me, man! You don't know what I'm feelin!" he belted, sounding like a straight female. "My fuckin girl done left me for a rat ass nigga and took my shorties, my O.G. been lyin to a nigga my whole life, and my pops been lyin too!" His words were coming out loud and slurred, making it almost impossible to hear what the fuck he was saying. If he added some tears, the nigga would have been Lifetime ready. I released my hold on him and he slid down the car, landing on his butt, like he couldn't handle standing up on his own. My face twisted in disgust at this nigga, out here clowning like this when there was work to put in. He hadn't even acted like this when I got shot.

"Nigga, you out here soundin like a straight up bitch! I'ma need you to pull yo fuckin self together!" I couldn't help but shake my head at this fool. He had went his whole life without a damn father and then wanted to breakdown when he finally got one, one that had technically been there the whole time from what he'd told me. I couldn't understand the logic of that shit but, then again, I hadn't had anybody since my people died. This seemed like some spoiled kid shit, and I was about to nip it in the bud. I pulled out my phone and called up Pree and mama Jackie, maybe they could come and fix this damn shit.

An hour or so later after I'd gotten this drunk ass nigga in the house, Pree finally pulled up with mama Jackie in his passenger seat. She ran over as soon as I opened the door and damn near pushed me out the way.

"Where's my baby!?" she huffed, frantically looking around the foyer like he was hiding somewhere in there.

"Damn ma, just fuck me, huh?" I can't lie, I felt a little slighted. Either she ain't hear me or she was ignoring the fuck outta me, as she headed into his living room and started fussing about him being laid out in there on the floor. Pree stepped inside, looking around at the house in appreciation, before bumping fists with me.

"Sup Pree," I greeted him and closed the door so that I could follow him into the living room.

"Wassup lil homie, thanks for givin us a call." I gave a quick nod as I fell into step beside him and we turned the corner and came up on Jackie hovering over a slumped Ju.

"I couldn't get through to his ass, so I figured I'd see if y'all could. Real shit though, if this what love do to a nigga, I don't ever want that shit!" I said, shaking my head at the sight before us and causing mama Jackie to look up at me angrily.

"Get up off my baby! Nivea is the first woman he's committed to."

I ain't know what she thought telling me that was gone do. I was still gone feel the same way about the shit. From my point of view, this nigga was out here soft as hell. Whatever Nivea had in her pussy had his ass looking like he would die without it, and I for damn sure ain't want no parts of some pussy that was gone have me looking like that. Hell, I was embarrassed for him.

"Move out the way Jack, let me get him to the shower," Pree finally said and tapped my arm to help him as she stood and moved to the side. We both bent down and I grabbed his feet, while Pree grabbed him underneath the arms. I felt bad for his ass too cause I knew his shit was gone be smelling musty as hell when we were through.

"Where the bathroom in this big muthafucka?" Pree questioned, looking at me with his face frowned up. The smell must have finally hit his nose. I shrugged cause this was my first time over here and I'd already forgotten where everything was from when I'd come in earlier.

"I don't know, but it gotta be like six of em up in here, but I ain't bouta carry his big ass up all them stairs."

"Fine, let me go look right quick," Mama Jackie said while rolling her eyes, but she wasn't the one holding his heavy ass. She stomped towards the back of the house and, after a few seconds, hollered that she had found one. Me and Pree headed in the direction of her voice and found her in a small hallway right by the kitchen. She pointed to a door on her left and we shuffled inside, placing Ju into the glass, stall shower. As soon as he was down, I flexed my back, trying to rid myself of the discomfort of having to carry that nigga's dead weight. For Ju to be so little, his ass was heavy as hell. Mama Jackie followed us inside, as Pree went to cut on the cold water.

"Wait, you not gone take his clothes off?" She frowned, causing Pree to stop with his hand outstretched to the faucet.

"This a grown ass man Jack. I ain't seen his dick since he was a baby, and I'd like to keep it that way."

"Well, I ain't never seen that shit, and I ain't tryin to either," I added, stepping back.

"Fine." She waved him off, and he proceeded to cut the water on before squatting down inside the door of the shower and slapping Ju's face a couple of times. It took a minute for him to react but, eventually, he came to and started swinging at nothing.

"Man, what the fuck!" He sat up and jumped away from the cold ass water. "Nigga, you put me in a fuckin cold shower?" His eyes landed on Pree and his scowl deepened. "Fuck is you doin here?"

"Trigga called me," Pree said simply, and Ju sought me out in the small bathroom, first finding mama Jackie and then me. He narrowed his eyes angrily and stood up unsteadily, causing Pree to reach out to try and help, but he pushed his hand away.

"Don't fuckin touch me!" he barked, and Pree put up both his hands in surrender. "Why the fuck you call them over here man!" He stomped out of the stall and almost slipped from how hard he was walking. I had to hold in a laugh at how ridiculous this nigga looked before answering.

"Shit nigga, you was out there damn near comatose, crying and shit, what the fuck was I sposed to do?" I ain't know what I was more pissed about; the fact that he was trying to flex on me or the fact that his ass hadn't stayed in the damn shower and added soap, but a nigga was pissed.

"Wasn't shit wrong with me! You was sposed to leave me the fuck alone! All y'all muthafuckas gotta get out!" he roared, pointing towards the door while everybody looked at his ass like the damn fool he was.

"I know you better pipe the fuck down when you talkin

to me and yo mama, nigga. You ain't seen it yet, but don't turn me into Supreme in this bitch."

"I don't give a fuck who yo ass is-" He was cut off by Pree grabbing his ass by his wet shirt and lifting him off of his feet. Mama Jackie screeched and ran over to try and get him off of Ju, while I just watched in damn awe. For one, Ju had been acting like a little bitch about finding out that Pree was his father and, for two, it was amazing to see an O.G. in the act. I was standing in the bathroom with hood royalty, shit was crazy.

"Let him down Jessiah!" she screamed, pulling at his arms, but Pree wasn't letting up his grip for nothing.

"Hell nah! This nigga need a lesson in manners, and I'm just the person to give it to him. This is why I told yo ass he needed his damn daddy around, Jackie; his lil ass out here disrespectful as fuck!"

"Well, comin in and fightin him ain't gone help either; now, put my baby down. You can talk to him without having to put your hands on him," she demanded, stomping her foot. This whole time, Ju was struggling to no avail because Pree's hold still hadn't loosened. If it was left up to me, his ass would have still been sitting up there for as long as Pree could hold him but, as it turned out, he was just as pussy whipped as his son. After a second or so, he let Ju down and turned to mama Jackie with a frown, as she checked Ju to make sure he was okay.

"Happy now?" he sneered.

"No, but I will be once my baby is sober and out here doin what he needs to do for this case to go away," she quipped and then brought her attention back to Ju. "Now Judah, I know you're mad about us not tellin you the truth, and Nivea losing her mind, but you need to put that shit on the back burner and focus on what's truly important right now, and that's yo freedom! I raised you better than this shit!

You are much stronger than your circumstances, and I need for you to pull through and go take care of this shit! Now, can you do that? If not for me, do it so that you don't become another statistic."

After a minute of staring at her staring him down, he finally nodded that he could. All it had taken was this nigga mama to say virtually the same shit I had already been saying to his ass. Either way though, it looked like my nigga was back and ready for some action, and I couldn't say that I wasn't geeked. I knew today wasn't gone be a good day to start since his ass needed to get himself together but, bright and early tomorrow, I planned on me and him painting the city red with blood. First, thing first though, I needed to make some other arrangements for tonight, even though I'd told Niyah to meet me at my crib; I just wasn't gone go home. I needed to slide into something new before Niyah had me out here looking like Ju's ass. She was already giving me forever vibes and I just wasn't ready for all that shit, especially if it had me showing out like my boy. Nope, I couldn't go out like that.

CHAPTER 6

*S*avage

My mama, Troy, and even Pree had all been right. I'd been sulking around this big ass house since Troy had dropped me off, getting drunk as fuck and high as hell. Then once I ran out of alcohol and shit, I drove my drunk ass to the store and got more. I knew that the most important thing was supposed to be me getting at those niggas Keys and Quad, but I couldn't help but to feel like a piece of me was missing. How was I supposed to move about the world when the biggest piece of my universe was missing? I felt betrayed as fuck. I'd done all the shit I was supposed to do and Nivea had basically turned her back on me. I would never admit it to nobody, but I was calling the fuck out of her that first night, only for her not to answer. The rational side of me figured that she was sleep; hell, it was two in the morning, but the most irrational side didn't want to believe that. That side was saying that she was in the middle of fucking and that's why she wasn't picking up. I was letting those damn depressing ass thoughts consume me to the point that I couldn't function. If Troy hadn't come when he did, there was no telling how much longer I would have drunk myself to death. Before he left, he made sure to tell me all the ill shit I had been saying and doing, and I told his ass he bet not ever bring that shit up again. Real talk, the stuff he told me I was screaming didn't even sound like me, but those were thoughts that I'd had, so I know more than likely that shit had come out my mouth.

"Here, eat this," my mama said, sitting a bowl of what looked like soup in front of me. Whatever that shit was it didn't even look edible, and I for damn sure wasn't about to eat it.

"Hell nah! If I eat that shit, I'ma throw up; it's the summertime anyway. Why the fuck you tryna give me soup?" I frowned, pushing the bowl away.

"Watch yo fuckin mouth Judah," she warned, slapping me on the back of my head and pulling the bowl back in front of me. "This a special recipe that my mama taught me to get rid of a hangover and, as drunk as yo ass was, you gone need it. Eat this first and I'll grab you somethin else when you finish."

"That shit ain't never worked Jackie. I'ma run out to the store and grab him some coffee and an omelet from IHOP."

"Don't talk about my mama shit, nigga. Every time I used it when I got too drunk, it worked." She dismissed what he was saying and he came further into the kitchen to stand across the island from her.

"That's cause you ain't never had no hangover girl, you can barely handle a mixed drink." My mama gasped like he'd just insulted her.

"Aye, I'm sittin right here man damn. I'm for real not eatin that shit ma, but I'll take the coffee and eggs Pree," I told him flatly. Me accepting his offer was the closest they were going to get to a truce from me.

"Bet." He threw my mama a look, and she shrugged and waved his ass off. It was starting to become clear that having two parents was more aggravating than anything. He started towards the door and I called out to him.

"Aye Pree!"

"No onions, right?" he asked, stopping without turning around to face me. I shot a look at my mama and she just shrugged again like 'duh nigga, of course he know what you allergic to'.

"Yeah," I finally got out, surprised that him knowing something like that about me had an effect on my hate for him. I watched him nod once, as he walked out of my sight and eventually the front door. My mama finally turned back to clean up the small mess she'd made in my kitchen, and I was glad that I'd decided to get some food and cleaning products before I was supposed to bring Nivea there the night of the show. In my mind, we were going to be living it up in here and she was gone be bringing a nigga's breakfast in bed. I guess that showed how much I knew. For now though, I couldn't afford to be thinking about Nivea or the kids. She'd made up her mind, well, technically she'd let another muthafucka make up her mind for her, but there wasn't shit I could do about that. Not until I got rid of Quad's hoe ass anyway and, since I couldn't do that at this moment, there was no point in thinking about it. Then, there was the situation with my O.G. and Pree. There was a lot of shit that I just couldn't understand with their whole story and, since my mama was right there, I may as well have asked her so that it came straight from the horse's mouth.

"So, you gone explain this shit between you and Pree with me, or y'all just gone keep actin like I ain't hear that he's my Pops?" I mused, prompting her to stop wiping down the counters.

"What do you want to know Judah?" her voice was shaky as hell, like she was scared of what I may ask, but that wasn't going to deter me.

"Shit, everything, how'd y'all meet? Why did he leave, hell, why'd you let him leave? Everything." I didn't want to miss shit about this story. Pretty much my whole life, my mama had been opposed to anything dealing with the streets and, come to find out, she was messing around with the biggest street nigga and possibly being his ride or die. She turned around and leaned against the counter top.

"Okay... well, I met Supre-, Jessiah in high school. He had just moved out here to stay with his Grand mama. Back then, I was... kinda wild so niggas sellin dope wasn't shit to me, but I hadn't met anybody on his level yet." She paused and looked off into space like she could see the shit playing in front of her. "I got caught up with him fast... doin shit I ain't have no business doin... and goin places I ain't have no business goin. Anyway, yo father was the first boy I can say that I really loved; I wanted to be up under him all the time and I was. I'd make his runs with him, and it even got to the point that I was out there toting guns and serving rocks with him. And then you came along," she paused and her eyes met mine.

"I ain't even find out I was pregnant until I was almost five months! I wasn't showing, I ain't have no morning sickness or nothin but, as soon as that test came back positive, I knew I couldn't keep runnin the streets behind yo daddy. I tried to get him to make the same sacrifice as me, but he just wasn't ready to leave the game alone. At first, I thought maybe if I gave him time, but one day we were leaving the doctor's office. Matter fact, it was the day we found out we were having a boy. He had this nice ass Bentley that was custom painted, candy apple red. He was the only one with a paint job like that around here, and everybody knew it was his car. Some niggas who he had gotten into it with saw us leaving the doctor and just opened fire on us! Right there in broad daylight! That was the first time I had been in a situation like that, and I was scared shitless! Your daddy wasn't scared though; he jumped right out and started shooting back, and I hadn't even known he had a gun on him. I must have been in shock cause I didn't even realize that I was shot until he came over to check on me."

"After that, I was done for real and I told him that if he didn't leave the streets alone, he would have to leave me and you alone cause I couldn't put you at risk again. He chose not to leave, and I'm assuming because he thought that I might change my mind or let him convince me to stay, but I just couldn't do that. I had more than just him and me to think about, and he wasn't ready to think about nobody but himself." I couldn't lie; her explaining the situation to me gave me a better understanding of why she didn't want me in the streets. Before this, she had only ever shown a disdain for it, never really going into detail about why. At the same time, the shit that Pree had been spitting to me the night I ran up on dude and his mama became even clearer, and I guess he was just trying to right his wrongs. I guess I could understand that too, but he still had a whole lot of making up to do. Especially for Janiah. Shit, I was grown and had lived through the years that I had needed him most. She still needed him to show her things that only a father could and he still had the chance to, if my mama would get out of her own way.

"So, what made you let him start comin back around for me and not Janiah?" I wanted to know, honestly confused. She had told me about her childhood without a father, so I guess I just didn't know why she would spare me, but not Janiah.

"Honestly, I just felt like at the time you needed him more. He's always been around on some level, you probably just don't remember, but he would try and wiggle his way back in. I only let him stop through here and there, but never once you were old enough to ask questions and stuff. The closer I saw you were getting to living the same life, the more I began to change my mind the effects of his presence on you." She shrugged. "Now Janiah, she had someone, she had me and I could at least teach her things about being a woman. But, you needed somebody to mold you into a man so, when I first saw you interested in rappin, I let Jessiah know, and his ass went and bought a whole freakin studio for you. Crazy ass nigga," she fussed and, again, it seemed like my mind was blown by Pree.

I'd figured all this time that my pops couldn't have cared about me, my sister, or my mama, just because he wasn't around when he had gone out of his way to involve himself in our lives. Fucking around with him, he had probably got my O.G. pregnant with Janiah just to have another tie to her. I nodded my head, silently unable to come up with any words for what I was feeling.

"So, I'ma assume that nod mean you understand that I wasn't tryna keep him from you, not necessarily anyway. I was more so protecting you from his ties to his activities." My mama looked my way with her brows raised as she posed the question in anticipation.

"Yeah ma, I get what you was tryna do and I can appreciate that so, I'll apologize for how I acted at the hospital but, real shit, Niah getting older and, whether you want to admit it or not, she *does* need him too." I let her know my thoughts and watched her face fill with understanding as she nodded.

"You're right, and we'll work on that, just as soon as we get you out this jam," she sassed, making me chuckle. Her ass swore she was hood.

"Brooooo, you can't be sayin shit like *that jam;* man, you too old for that!" I laughed, and she gave me a crazy look.

"Boy, I was getting outta jams before it was called that! Now, what you tryna do bout this nigga, cause he gotta go."

"I guess I came back at the right time," Pree said, walking into the kitchen and sitting the IHOP bag on the counter. "Gone head eat, then we can discuss a plan and, at some point after all this shit die down, we gone talk man to man." He stuck his hand out for a shake, calling a truce to our drama, but I was already over it since I understood their point of view on things; still, I guess it wouldn't hurt to hear his side too.

"Bet," I agreed and bumped his fist. Satisfied with my answer, he took a seat next to me while I tore into my food and, with my O.G. on standby, we went over our next moves.

CHAPTER 7

*S*aniyah
  It had been a few days since I'd last talked to Troy's ass after he sent me off at his crib. I wasn't really tripping too hard; I just didn't like my time being wasted, but he would soon learn that. I was giving him the benefit of the doubt though and assuming that something with Ju came up, but that wasn't going to stop me from not calling his ass. A part of me felt like if it had been an emergency, then it shouldn't have been a problem to simply call and let me know, but his ass just stayed gone the whole fucking night. And to make it worse, he still hadn't shown up by the next afternoon.

  YEP! You guessed it! I. Me. Saniyah Monique Smith had waited there for his ass. Hmph! This shit was grounds for termination on his part, but I couldn't just cut him loose. As hard as it was to admit it, Troy had me pressed like a suit fresh from the dry cleaners! He'd never know it though, if I could help it.

  I was pretty sure he was used to girls sweating him and giving up the ass whenever he wanted, especially since they'd signed their contracts, but I wasn't one of these other thirst bucket ass hoes! I thought he knew that, but I guess not.

Even though I wanted to text or call him to curse his ass out, I was gone let him make it; besides, I had more important things to do. Like going to see my mama. As I drove through traffic, I tried to call Nivea for what felt like the hundredth time and it went straight to voicemail again. I wasn't surprised. I'd just pop up on her ass later, cause her ass was acting like since she broke shit off with Ju, she was breaking up with me too. There may have been legalities that stopped him from coming around, but wasn't nothing to stop me from going over there. Besides, I hadn't even seen my God babies cause of Quad's bitch ass and that was a problem for me.

Once I pulled in front of my mama's house, I rolled my eyes at the sight of her friend, Sister Marie's, car parked in the driveway. I already knew it was about to be some shit because this lady always had something to say and, every time she said something to me, I said something right back. My mama usually tried to keep us away from each other, but she wasn't expecting my visit today. I made my way up the porch and knocked on the door hard, knowing that they were probably in the dining room in the back of the house.

"Who is it?" my mama's voice trilled from behind the door, and I huffed irritably.

"It's me ma!" I heard the many locks coming undone and then the door swung open, revealing my mama standing there with an attitude.

"You couldn't just say yo name Saniyah? Me could have been anybody, hell." She immediately started fussing me out, but I knew she knew my voice and she knew black people ain't like saying their name at the door.

"It couldn't be just anybody callin you Ma. I'm your only kid," I teased, planting a kiss on her cheek as I walked past her and into the house. She didn't have an argument for that because it was true. My mama had made it all the way to forty with no husband, or man to speak of. She claimed that I was the result of a one-night stand and, since I was her first pregnancy, she decided to take the risk and have me. I grew up with no father around; I'd never met the man and I wasn't pressed to about it either. My mama had went above and beyond to raise me and give me everything my heart desired, which was one of the main reasons that I was so high maintenance. I respected my mother for every sacrifice she had ever made for me and I hoped that I could be at least half of the woman she was.

"Where you goin all dressed up?" she questioned, her mood lightened by the kiss. I looked down at the nude Fashion Nova tank dress and tan Fenty sandals I wore with a slight frown.

"My only plans were to come visit you and then go see Niv for a bit, but this is hardly dressed up," I told her with a shrug.

"Well, you could stand to put a lil more on if you asked me." I hadn't noticed Sister Marie slither her old ass into the room but, the minute she spoke, I needed to take a few calming breathes.

"Well, it's a good thing nobody asked yo old ass, huh?" I sneered. Can you believe that this bitch clutched her chest like she hadn't come for me first?

"Watch your mouth Saniyah!" my mama chastised.

"Sorry ma, but you know I ain't bouta just let her say anything to me. I'll quit though, if she does." Our eyes fell on Marie and I could tell her old ass wanted to say some more smart shit.

"I was just saying that she should respect herself by having on more clothes Sharon, ain't no man gone buy the cow when he can get the milk for free!"

"See! This the shit I'm talkin bout! Would you rather me be like your dumb ass daughter, the one that's married but be gettin her ass beat on the regular! Only reason she wears so many clothes is cause she tryna hide the bruises, and the only reason your other daughter stay covered up is so yo ass can't see the track marks on her arms! Why don't you go parent them cause I'm good over this way!"

By now, the lady was almost in tears from finding out the truth about her raggedy ass kids. If she was busy minding their business, instead of mine, then she would have known already.

"You gone just let her talk to me like that?" She turned to my mama with wide eyes and was disappointed to see her shrug.

"You the one kept that shit up Marie; she told you she was gone from it and you just couldn't leave well enough alone."

"Well, if that's how you feel, then I think I'm gone leave." Marie huffed, gathering up the fake, worn out MK purse I was sure one of her bum ass sons had given her.

"Okay, bye! You ain't did nothin but sit over here and talk about Deacon Young's wife this whole time anyway!" My mama waved her ass on and slammed the door behind her.

"Anyway, where the food at mama?" I asked while sitting down on the couch, completely unbothered by the fact that I had run her annoying ass friend off.

"Ain't no damn food girl, you done made my ride to the grocery store leave, so now you gotta take me." She stood over me with her hands on her hips.

"If I do, are you gone cook?"

"Don't I always cook when you bring yo lil worrisome ass over here?" I couldn't help the huge grin that plastered my face as I hopped right up and threw my shades back on. I loved my mama's cooking and, considering that my ass could barely boil water, I was glad that she was still willing to cook me a whole meal whenever I decided to pop up on her. She shuffled around the living room getting her stuff together and, then, we finally left.

Two hours later, we were finally pulling back up to her house. She had made sure to grab her enough damn food to last her for two months instead of just getting something to cook, and a bitch was dumb heated. So, you could imagine that at the sight of my shady ass cousin standing on her porch with her two kids, I was ready to go off. I left my mama right in the car talking about how nice it was to see her only niece with the nastiest scowl on my face.

"Heyyyy cuzzin-" she started to say, but I waved my hand and cut her dumb ass off.

"Bitch, don't hey cuzzin me! You got yo nerve comin over here like you ain't start all that damn shit!" I looked down at my cousins and my frown deepened at the sight of them dressed in some too little ass clothes that were out of season, with their hair all over their heads. "And how the fuck you get these damn kids back?" Kisha looked shocked by my outburst, but she knew we hadn't been tight for a long ass time.

When we were younger, we were real close considering that my mama and her mama were sisters and we were the only girls in a sea of boy cousins. We were close enough to be sisters and were always at the other's house; hell, we even dressed alike. Around the time that we hit our teenage years though, we started to grow apart. While I was trying to excel in school and wasn't too much into boys, her ass ended up dropping out when she found out she was pregnant with my first baby cousin Kenasia. I started back fucking with her after that, thinking that I should have been helping her instead of shunning her, but obviously the bitch ain't have an "act right" bone in her body. Besides the fact that she was abusive as hell towards the baby and her child's father

55

Kenyon, she was neglectful and dirty as hell. The little two bedroom apartment that he'd managed to get for them stayed filthy and all she ever wanted to do was party.

That didn't stop Kenyon from impregnating her dumb ass again not too long after Kenasia turned one and, by then, I'd stopped coming around as much because I just couldn't watch the self-destruction they had going on over there. Thankfully though, Kenyon left her not too long after she delivered Kenisha and they'd been with their father ever since. So, to see them with her right now didn't sit right with me at all.

"What you even talkin bout startin shit? I ain't started nothin and it ain't none of yo business what I'm doin with MY kids!"

"Yeah, okay! Play that slow role if you want too! I owe you an ass whoopin already bitch, don't make it two! You know good and damn well that you ain't sposed to have these kids!" I snapped, causing her to take a step back away from me.

"Niyah, leave that girl alone! She don't need to be gettin all stressed out while she pregnant! I invited her and the girls here for dinner and I ain't tryna have you run them off like you did Marie!" my mama fussed as she came up the stairs. Hearing that Kisha was supposed to be pregnant had me looking down at her flat stomach. Either her ass was lying or she had just gotten popped off; for the baby's sake, I prayed that she was lying though.

"Ma, you know she ain't got custody of these kids-"

"Saniyah! I don't care. I just want to make sure that they eat! That's more important than any of that other shit." She cut me off, bringing a slick ass smirk to Kisha's face, and I held in the desire to slap it off. My mama was right though. The kids getting some food was a top priority, especially since there was no telling when the last time they'd gotten a meal was.

"Fine ma." I brushed past them both and went to grab some bags out of the car, while she let them inside of the house. Kenyon took damn good care of those girls, so I really wanted to know how they ended up with Kisha, looking hungry and like they hadn't bathed in a couple of days. Best believe I was going to find out a way to get in contact with him to find out what was going on.

CHAPTER 8

*N*ivea

It had been a couple of days since the kids had come home, and the only one who had warmed up to Quad was Quiana. QJ was acting like he didn't want nothing to do with his ass, and Kymia's nasty ass attitude had come back with a vengeance, mainly only when his ass was around. I'd tried to talk to her about what was going on and she didn't have much to say to me about the situation, always telling me that nothing was wrong. I decided to back off, but I was going to keep an eye on her.

Quad was still making some funny moves though and, while I had yet to say anything about it, I was watching his ass too. He thought I didn't know about the weird ass phone calls he was taking into the other room. I pretended not to be too worried about the constant disappearing acts too. The day we'd left my mama's house, he had me drop him off at the train station on 95th. That in itself was odd as hell to me because as far as I knew, his ass didn't know anybody around there, but I was starting to learn that Quad had a bunch of secrets that he'd kept from me.

Today was my first day back to work since before Judah's show and I was scared as hell to face Jackie. I knew that Judah hadn't been talking to her, but I was also sure that she still knew about all that was going on. I slowly put on my uniform shirt and pulled my hair into my signature ponytail as I listened to the kids run around the living room. Quad was out there with them watching t.v. or at least trying to with all the noise they were making. He'd pretty much given up on trying to gain their affection back and was only putting forth an effort with Quiana, which seemed to be fine with Ky and QJ, but the shit irritated the fuck out of me.

"Hey, you bouta cook somethin?" Quad came into the room and asked before he realized what I had on and his face frowned up. "Wait, where you goin?"

I tried not to roll my eyes at him just busting up in my room without knocking. He knew I didn't like that because I had told him on more than one occasion not to do the shit. I'd thought I had made it clear that we weren't moving that way, but he still insisted on putting up a front like we were together.

"To work," I told him simply, not wanting to hold too much of a conversation. His ass was really working my damn nerves and I was regretting letting him stay with me already.

"Fuck is you goin back to work for that nigga mama for?" he raised his voice.

"Why wouldn't I?" I stopped primping and turned my body away from the mirror to fully face him.

"Plenty of fuckin reasons! One, being that you might run into that crazy ass nigga up there; hell, his mama bout be the one to call him and tell him you there!" he shrieked.

"First of all, you need to lower your voice, and I already told you to watch how you talk to me." I looked past him to make sure none of the kids had come down this way since he was being so loud. "Jackie been helpin me long before me and Judah even got together! I ain't bouta quit just cause you don't want me around him! How the fuck you sound!" He looked at me with his head tilted and narrowed his eyes before nodding.

"Yeah, you right. Let me get a ride then cause I ain't bouta stay here and babysit while you out workin," he spat out the word like it tasted bad in his mouth. I couldn't believe him! His ass was so pressed about Judah that he wanted me to sit around there unemployed, but he wasn't trying to bring no money in. Then, he didn't even want to babysit either!

"Ain't nobody say you was bouta watch MY kids! My mama been keepin them while I work for the last fuckin three years, ain't shit changed cause you popped up!" I sassed. I was sick of him talking all reckless and shit like I needed him, when the truth of the matter was that he needed me more. His neck snapped back like I had slapped him and his face darkened. Before I could do or say anything, he was in the room with his hands around my throat.

"Bitch! Is you crazy! That lil nigga got you smellin yoself? You been talkin real fuckin stupid to me ever since I touched down!" he screamed in my face as his hands tightened. I tried to claw at his fingers as I struggled to get some air in, but he had a death grip on me.

"St-stoppp," I managed to gasp, but it was like he was in a zone. His eyes glazed over as he brought his face closer to mine.

"Yeah, yo ass ain't got shit to say now huh! The whole reason I was gone for three years is cause I was tryna take care of you and yo kids!" he continued his rant, shooting spit out of his mouth with each word.

I could feel myself about to lose consciousness and I struggled to get out of his grasp. He was more upset than the night he'd shown up here and that had to be the maddest I'd ever seen him until right now. I mean, sure, he'd hemmed me up before or raised his voice and made threats, but he had never put his hands on me like this. I honestly thought I was about to lose my life in this room. My body was growing weaker, and my eyelids were fluttering closed when he finally just let me drop to the floor. I turned over onto my side, coughing as I tried to suck in as much air as I could without vomiting. All of the kids ran over to me and sat asking questions, and I realized that they were the reason that he'd finally let me go. He stood over by the dresser with not one ounce of regret on his face, before he stormed off and I heard the unmistakable sound of the front door slamming shut. Quiana and QJ were both crying hysterically while Kymia sat off to the side looking at me in pity. Suddenly, I was glad that I couldn't speak because I didn't know what to say to them. How was I supposed to explain their father sitting in here choking me damn near to the point of unconsciousness?

I had messed up a lot over the years, but I prided myself on the mother that I'd become. My children witnessing me being abused was never something I thought I would allow to happen and, now that it had, I didn't know what to do. I was still literally shaking as I tried to soothe them and catch my breath at the same time. *You need to get up and get the kids out of here before he comes back Nivea!* I mentally coached myself and, after another minute or so, I was able to stand.

"Lis- listen, it's okay… mommy's okay, but I need y'all to get up and put on some clothes as fast as you can, ok?" my voice came out shaky and hoarse, as I helped QJ and Quiana up off of the floor and then turned my attention to Kymia, who was just staring off into space. "Kymia! I need you to go and help them get ready and pack some clothes… enough for a few days!" I raised my voice a bit to snap her out of her trance and she moved to go and do what I told her.

Once all of the kids had left the room, I hurried to throw

61

a few of my own things into an overnight bag. I didn't trust that Quad wouldn't come back and I wasn't about to play games with my life. My hands shook as I dialed up Niyah with one hand and threw clothes in the bag with the other but, after calling her three times and not getting an answer, I gave up. The most important thing at this moment was getting the fuck up out of there; I could figure out the rest later.

"I'm done ma."

Kymia stood in my doorway with Quiana and QJ each holding their book bags that looked stuffed.

"You got underwear and socks, right?" I asked, trying to think if there was anything else we might have forgot.

"Yeah, enough for a week." She nodded and I realized that although she may have been upset about the situation, she seemed okay with us leaving. I didn't waste time thinking too hard on it though. After I made sure I was all packed, I double checked for my important papers that I carried in my purse and we damn near ran up out of there.

I don't know why but, instead of going to my Mama's house, I ended up pulling up in front of Jackie's bakery. Maybe it was because I didn't want to hear my mama go on and on about how she had told me so, but I knew that it was the fact that I felt safe there. I wiped the fresh set of tears from my face and turned to the kids who had been extremely quiet the entire ride. Quiana, who usually was a ball of questions, was silently looking out of the window, not even peaked to say anything about the fact that we were at the bakery, which had become one of her favorite places. I knew that she would probably be the one most affected by what had happened because despite his bullshit, she loved Quad to death. Seeing him bringing harm to me more than likely had her thinking all types of shit. QJ thankfully was sleeping, and that was probably another reason that the ride had been so quiet, and Kymia had her headphones on while looking out of the window.

Again, I was at a loss for words. I didn't know how to explain this situation to them and I was sure I never would. Finally, I just released a sigh and told them to come on. The girls went ahead inside, while I got QJ out of his car seat and then followed them in. The bell over the door rang as I stepped through and saw Jackie sitting some cake on top of one of the booths for the girls. She looked up at me and, without saying a word, came over and wrapped me up into a hug. I stood there as another wave of emotion hit me and more tears spilled out, while QJ drooled on my shoulder. When she finally released me, I could see her eyes were moist too, but she didn't let a tear fall.

"I see somebody's lil big mouth self filled you in?" I chuckled bitterly, shooting a glare Quiana's way.

"Tuh! Leave that baby alone, I woulda knew anyway. Hell, yo neck gave you away too." She shrugged. My hand immediately went to my neck; I hadn't even thought about the fact that he'd left bruises on me. "Come in the back, so you can lay him down and we can talk." She took me by the hand and started pulling me toward her office without waiting for me to say yes.

Once I had QJ laid down on the couch, me and Jackie sat in the chairs that she had in front of her desk.

"Now, first things first, did you call the police on that lil piece of shit?" she asked, cupping my hands in hers.

"No, I just left. I've never really been in a situation like that and I don't know if the police will even do anything, since he's supposed to be a witness." She nodded her understanding and then leaned closer.

"Have you tried to call Judah?" My eyes bucked at the question and I shook my head emphatically.

"Hell no, he don't want nothin to do with me right now,

I'm sure he told you what happened," I said, unable to meet her eyes. I wasn't sure what Jackie knew about the situation and I didn't know what she thought of me, but she made it clear when she smacked her lips and waved away what I'd said.

"Girl, that boy *loves* you. None of that old shit matters; the second you tell him what happened, he's gonna come runnin."

"But... I..."

"You believed what the police and your baby daddy said," she finished my sentence, and I nodded stiffly.

"Listen, I think you need to give him a chance to explain his side of the story. You gave Quad that chance but denied it to Judah, when you yourself have to admit that the reasoning and the accusers just don't make any sense."

I thought about what she was saying and realized that maybe I had jumped the gun by immediately believing in Judah's guilt, when Quad was actually being the most suspect. Me and Judah hadn't known each other that long but, in the time that we had spent together, he'd become pretty reliable and predictable. While I was with Quad for years, I was still learning things about him. Seeing the realization on my face, Jackie smiled for the first time since I'd walked in.

"See! Gone head and call your man girl!"

CHAPTER 9

*Q*uad

    I really hadn't meant to put my hands on Nivea. It wasn't some shit that I was used to doing, but her mouth was getting more and more reckless lately. I didn't know what that nigga Savage had done to her, but she wasn't the easy going, quiet Niv that I had left a few years ago. Now, her ass was extra, and she ain't give a damn what she said to a nigga. How he could put up with that shit, I would never know, but having her talk down on me was one thing. Having her talking crazy right after I had gotten a phone call that Keys was missing was something completely different.

"It's about time you brought yo ass home!" Desiree stood in the doorway with her arms folded, blocking me from entering.

"I ain't bouta do this shit with you, man; either you gone let me in or I'ma go back to my baby mama crib," I threatened, even though I knew damn well I couldn't go back there, not right now anyway. I turned around like I was about to leave and, just like I knew she would, she grabbed my arm to stop me.

"Okay! Okay, don't leave."

I allowed her to pull me back and into the apartment like she'd really convinced me to stay, when the truth was I didn't have a choice. To keep up the front, I pretended to have an attitude as she wrapped her arms around me and planted kisses along my neck.

"I just missed you, bae; I'm sorry." She pressed her body further into mine and placed my hands on her ass since I'd still been holding them down at my sides, but I grabbed her by the wrist instead and pushed her away from me.

"Why the fuck is Keys missin?" I wanted to know. Her face registered confusion and then shock, before she cocked her head to the side.

"What do you mean missing?"

"Bitch! I mean exactly what I said! The nigga missin!" I exploded angrily.

"That doesn't make any sense, he was in witness protection-"

"Exactly! Y'all was sposed to keep that nigga safe and couldn't even do that! And you wonder why the fuck I ain't tryna go in that shit! Savage probably got some fuckin police officers helpin him!" I wasn't putting nothing past that little mutha fucka! Keys had put his life in the hands of the jakes and he was gone. I could bet the fifty dollars in my pocket that his ass was dead, and I wasn't about to let that shit happen to me.

"Don't be ridiculous, CPD wouldn't have shit to do with somebody like him," Desiree scoffed, waving her hand like I was stupid.

"You sound dumb as fuck right now, just shut the fuck up!" I paced the small living room, trying to think of anywhere that I could go.

"You need to calm down Quad-"

"Don't fuckin tell me to calm down! Call them fuckin

detectives right now!" She looked irritated by the request and me constantly interrupting her, but she picked up her cell phone from the table and dialed a number. "Put that shit on speaker." Rolling her eyes, she pressed the screen and the room filled with the loud sound of the phone ringing before somebody finally picked up.

"Detective Ross."

"Hey detective, I have Quad here and-"

"And I wanna know what the fuck y'all gone do to protect me God dammit!" I yelled.

"Um, Quad, first things first, you need to calm down-"

"Stop fuckin tellin me to calm down! Where the fuck y'all niggas at!" Fed up, I snatched the phone from her hand and began pacing with it.

"Listen, yelling at me isn't going to get the desired effect for you, son. Now, we already have eyes on you and have done so since you walked out of that prison. No one is going to get to you, trust me on that."

"Oh, trust you like Keys did!"

"Hey, that lil stupid punk decided to do a show! Him disappearing didn't have shit to do with us, it was his fucking ego that got him where he is! Don't let yours be your down fall too!" he warned and then the line went silent, indicating that he had hung up. I didn't know that the reason that Keys was missing was because he had went to a fucking show. That was dumb as hell, considering that he knew the only person who could link Savage to the crime was him. I released a sigh and plopped down on the couch with Desiree's phone still wrapped tightly in my hand. Since the key witness was out, it was left up to me and all I had to do was lay low until everything blew over. I'd been sitting up under Nivea because I knew that Savage wouldn't risk it with her around, but now that shit was dead and Desiree was my last option.

"Now, see, there's nothing to worry about." She came around the front of the couch and cooed, gently taking her phone from my hand. Now that relief had set in, I could pay a bit more attention to the skimpy fishnet romper that she wore. I didn't object, even though she still didn't know that I'd choked Nivea damn near to death. As crazy as she was, she probably wouldn't have gave a fuck anyway. She slowly snaked her way between my legs and released my hard dick from the cover of my jeans. "This right here is all you need to concern yourself with." I smirked as she ran her tongue up and down my length. Yeah. This was all I needed to worry about at the moment and, later, I would convince her to get me a couple of guns so that I could take care of Savage myself, since he seemed to be so fucking elusive. I'd make sure to fuck the shit out of Desiree's face and pussy in the meantime, since I couldn't do the shit to Nivea.

CHAPTER 10

Kisha

I sat in my car watching, as Savage and Pree strolled into his mama's bakery with his little sister in tow. I'd been following his ass for a week now and still hadn't found the right time to approach him with our little family. The way I saw it playing out in my head, he would be alone, which would probably make him a little more approachable but, as it was, he was constantly with someone. With those charges being brought against him, he probably felt better having at least one person with him at all times. Now, while I wasn't happy about that, the bright side was that I hadn't seen him with that bitch Nivea at all, which was perfect for me. I didn't know what was going on with them, but in the grand scheme of things, them being apart would work in my favor.

"I'm hungry Kisha," my oldest Kenasia whimpered from the backseat. I briefly glanced at her annoying ass in the rearview and rolled my eyes. Would it have killed her slow ass to call me mama? For as long as I could remember, she'd never called me anything other than my name, but that shit was going to have to change once I got back with Savage. He struck me as the type to not like children disrespecting their mama.

"I just fed y'all Kenasia, damn is you always hungry?" I'd only had them for not even a month and they were already getting on my nerves. I real shit didn't know how Kenyon had done it by himself all these years and, if it hadn't been too late to take them back, I would have. Besides, Savage would probably be more willing to take care of the baby in my stomach since it was his... well, I hoped it was anyway.

"That was when we woke-"

"I don't give a fuck when it was! At least you ate something, hell, if you was smart, you would have saved some for later." I shrugged. She was lucky; there was starving kids in Africa who wasn't eating at all and she wanted to cry because she didn't get *more* food. At four, she probably didn't have the mental capacity to consider saving food for later, but that wasn't my fault. Of course, in spoiled kid fashion, she started to cry.

"Girrrrl, what's wrong with yo ass now?" I snapped. I wasn't in the mood for the bullshit today. Niyah had been blowing Kenyon's phone up since she saw me at her mama house the week before trying to dry snitch, but little did she know I had that nigga's phone and there was no way she would be able to get in contact with him, not where he was at anyway. After me pretending to be him and telling her that I had permission to get the girls, she still made it her business to continue texting and calling on Facebook, which was already annoying in itself. Once I saw that she wasn't going to leave me the fuck alone, I quickly introduced her to his block list.

"I want to go hooomme," she cried out, acting like a straight brat and, of course, her sister decided to join in.

"Naw, you want a whoopin is what you want! I told you

that yo daddy wants y'all to stay with me cuz he's sick! Y'all stuck with me until he gets better!" The more I said that lie, the easier it became. See, the truth was that that they'd never go home again, and they weren't gonna be seeing their daddy anymore either. It was honestly still hard to believe that Kenyon was dead, and even harder to comprehend that I was the one who'd killed him. It wasn't like I had done it on purpose though; I'd really just wanted to come and take my daughters.

When I'd called myself getting out of dodge all those months ago, I had set out to gain custody of my girls. I figured that since Savage's ass was into bitches with kids, then seeing that I had two would at least give me some type favor with him. The only thing was that I'd have to trick my slow ass baby daddy into giving them to me, since everybody thought I was such a danger to them. When me and Kenyon met in high school, he was a complete bitch for me and did whatever I told him to, which was the main reason I even paid him any attention but, once our daughter was born, he channeled everything towards Kenasia. At first, me doing little stuff to her here and there was because I resented her for taking the spotlight off me, but then I realized that I just didn't like her much and I damn sure didn't like being a mother.

So, when that faulty ass implant failed and I got pregnant with Kenisha, I wanted to die. Kenyon, who had watched me struggle with motherhood, didn't care at all how I felt about it either, he wanted the baby. I guess he thought that I could learn to love and take care of them properly but, once he found out that I was hurting her too, his ass left me! He didn't even try to get me help or nothing! Proof of E.R. visits and witness statements were all it took for them to give him full custody of our kids, but I didn't even care; I wanted to be free. The judge tried to tell me that I could have gotten jail time but, since postpartum was such a serious illness, he decided against it. I wanted so bad to let him know that I didn't have that shit but, if it kept me out of jail, I was willing to let them think whatever they wanted.

I felt like getting rid of the kids and Kenyon's worrisome ass was a new start at life. Without them holding me back, it had become easy to get back into my old interests, which included music and partying. It had taken awhile to hook up with Savage but, since I had, I hadn't thought about Kenyon or our kids until now.

The plan had been to go back to Kenyon and pretend that I wanted our family back, then somehow get him to sign the girls over to me. I spent three damn months trying to convince him that I was "mother material". It wasn't enough though. Not for Kenyon anyway, so I figured I would use what I always did when I wanted my way with him. Good old fashioned pussy.

Everything started out fine. I made them all Hamburger Helper for dinner and, since I'd spiked the girls' juice with some Benadryl, they were out not too long after eating. Since the cocktail that I'd used on Savage had worn off fast as hell, I upped the dosage for Kenyon, but I must have used way too much because his ass was breathing funny as hell and shaking before I even had a chance to pull the custody papers out. I couldn't call the ambulance and get in no trouble, so I thought that maybe he could sleep it off. Eventually, he stopped shaking and his breathing slowed down, so I guided his hand over the signature line on the paper. It wasn't perfect, but it would do. Satisfied, I left him in the living room and went to bed with a smile on my face knowing that he would be none the wiser about what had happened when he woke up, but he never woke up.

The next morning, I came out of the bedroom to find him lying in the same spot, cold and stiff as hell. Once I realized his ass was dead, I panicked and grabbed what I could from the apartment, which included his debit card and any cash he had. With the girls in tow, I left, telling them that he was sick and we would just come back when he was feeling better. Him being dead was actually a way better way to obtain custody of the kids and, honestly, suicide wasn't too farfetched for Kenyon's slow ass. Considering that I wasn't involved with him or the girls, nobody would suspect me and I would just say that we had visitation set up so the girls were with me when he killed himself. Now, I was regretting getting these whiny ass kids.

"Shut y'all asses up before I really give y'all something to cry about!" I threatened and they both snapped their mouths shut, knowing what I was capable of. Turning my attention back to the bakery, I realized that Savage must have left because his car was gone. They'd fucked around and made me miss him, and now I was pissed all the way off. I reached back and slapped the shit out of both of them. "Look what you made me fuckin do!"

I was livid! Now, I would have to drop them off with my Aunty. Maybe it would be better anyway if I showed up alone and eased him into everything else. I angrily started my car and drove off.

There wasn't too many places that I knew of to look for Ju. Honestly, I'd gotten lucky when I found out where he lived before, and I was surprised that he'd even let me in a couple months ago without pressing me on how I knew his address. But, he didn't live there anymore. That had been the first place I'd gone to when I came back with the girls. I only knew where he was from following Troy's dumb ass around because they weren't even using the same studio but, of all the damn places he led me to, Ju's new house wasn't one of them. It wasn't like I could follow either of them niggas around all day with two kids with me all the time. This whole plan was starting to seem dumb as hell, but I couldn't give up now. I'd done way too much and put in too much time to just not follow through with this. I was going to be the woman on his arm, and I was going to be the one reaping the benefits and bragging rights of being Ju Savage's bitch.

All I had to do was just hang in there a little bit longer and come up with a better plan. The girls had finally cried themselves to sleep and I was thankful as hell because I was close to putting a pillow over both of their faces if they hadn't shut up soon. I needed quiet to think and the ride back to the raggedy ass motel room gave me just enough time.

CHAPTER 11

*T*roy

"Aye! Run that back one mo time!" Ju said from inside the booth. I nodded and pressed the button to rewind the track as I pulled from my blunt. We had been working damn near nonstop on the album. And while we hadn't had any good news as far as our enemies went, we still had been winning when it came to our music. At first, the label was ready to drop Ju's ass because they wasn't trying to invest money in a nigga that might have been going to jail but, after seeing how his sales blew up after the arrest, they quickly changed their minds. On top of being in the studio nonstop, they were booking us for local shows since Ju couldn't leave Chicago. And when we weren't on the come up, we were combing the streets for Keys and trying to come up with a way to discreetly get at Quad.

We didn't have very much time before Ju would be hauled back off to court though, and I would have preferred to get the shit taken care of sooner rather than later. Pree had even gotten out here and was putting in work, but it ain't seem like he was having any luck either.

The song was coming to a close and I leaned forward so that I could fade him out, as the door to the studio swooshed open. I choked on the smoke I'd just inhaled at the sight of Niyah standing before me with Nivea coming in behind her.

"Hey Troy," she said smoothly, before leaning over the sound board and pressing the button to speak to Ju, who was still in the booth staring at Nivea, even though the song was over.

"Shit, wassup," I spoke back, trying to sound as casual as she had, despite the burning in my throat, but she was already speaking to Ju.

"Heeeyyy Ju! Bring yo ass out here and talk to my girl!" I couldn't stop myself from eyeing her body. Her ass was looking good as hell in some little ass gray drawstring shorts, with a matching gray cutoff top, and a jean jacket, and on her feet were a pair of gray and pink true flights. I'd never seen a female make a pair of Jordan's look as sexy as she had that day. I hadn't talked to her since the morning I'd sent her off, but seeing her now made me realize that I'd missed her little short ass. She had surprised me by not hitting me up at all this last week, and I wasn't used to shit like that. Females usually hounded me, especially after I gave them some dick, but not Niyah. She was playing the shit real cool and that wasn't sitting right with me.

"Sup Niv?" I finally tore my eyes away from Niyah's ass long enough to say. She gave me a small wave but never stopped looking in the booth at Ju. I was guessing that he still hadn't said shit to her or made an attempt to leave out so they could talk because she was standing there stuck looking like she wanted to cry, and he was in there mugging hard as hell.

"I ain't fuckin with shorty right now Niyah," he dismissed her and then brought his attention to me. "Play that track back Trigga."

Nivea nodded solemnly with tears glistening her eyes, but Niyah was pissed; she stood there with her arms folded, glaring at Ju. The whole shit had me uncomfortable as hell to be honest. As fucked up as he was when his ass couldn't get to her, he should have been running out the booth so they could talk, but that relationship shit was tricky as hell. I could see now he called himself trying to hurt her back and I couldn't do shit but shake my head.

"Nigga, we just finished that shit... come talk to yo girl." He stubbornly stayed where he was and adjusted his headphones like I hadn't said shit. I wasn't gone put my boy out there like that and blast him for the episode at his crib, but I damn sure wanted to ask him why he'd done all that crying and shit for if he wasn't gone talk to her when she finally came around.

"Forget it Niyah, let's just go," she finally huffed.

"Hell nah, his ass see you out here and I know he miss you just as much as you miss his bright ass!" Niyah sneered. "And look at yo fuckin neck, bitch!" Nivea's mouth dropped open and I was sure if she could have, she would've turned bright red from embarrassment, but Niyah got the desired effect because Ju was out of the booth in a flash.

"What the fuck wrong with yo neck!" he barked, damn near pushing Niyah out the way. I sat watching shit play out like a soap opera while I finished off my blunt. Ju was all in Nivea's shit inspecting her neck and he must have found what Niyah was talking about because he tilted her head hard as hell and took a closer look.

"What the fuck happened to yo shit Niv!" She looked like she didn't want to say anything for fear of making him more mad but, little did she know, the damage was done.

"I tried to call you, Judah... it wasn't like I wanted Quad to be there; we been gettin' into it anyway and..."

"You don't know what I been through these last couple

days. Rodnie tried to rape me in front of JoJo and he was screamin daddy and I was there by myself!" I said, making my voice sound like I was about to cry like Taraji P. Henson in 'Baby Boy'. I must have been high as hell, but this shit was just like that scene at P's house, and I damn near had tears in my eyes from laughing so hard. Everybody in the room looked my way though with a straight face, like they ain't get what I was saying.

"What, y'all don't get it?" I questioned with a raised brow, and Niyah just shook her head at me.

"We get it, that shit just ain't funny."

I waved her ass off while Ju pulled Nivea out into the hallway to talk, leaving us alone. Niyah sat down in the swivel chair next to me and immediately pulled out her phone and started scrolling through it like I wasn't even sitting there. She was really trying to act unbothered by a nigga. I threw what little of the blunt I had left in the ashtray and grabbed ahold of her chair, pulling her between my legs and snatching her phone away. She ain't even put up a fight, just sat back with her arms folded and a bored look covering her face.

"So, yo ass can't speak Niyah?"

"Boy, I spoke to you when I came in," she dismissed, rolling her eyes.

"Be easy with that boy shit Niyah, you know I'm all man over here."

"Oh, so leavin me at yo crib and not hittin me up to say you not comin is man shit?" She cocked her head to the side and the smirk I wore dropped. I wasn't expecting her to bring that shit up but, since she had, I was gone flip shit on her.

"Shiiit, you know what I'm out here tryna do, some shit came up and I couldn't make it." I shrugged, sitting back myself. She didn't seem like she believed that lie though.

"You couldn't call or send a bitch a text. I would have understood, that ain't the real reason you sent me off tho. I thought we was better than that, if you wanted to fuck with somebody else, you could have said that shit; it ain't like we exclusive."

"I just told you what I was doin, and fuck you mean not exclusive! We as exclusive as shit get!" Her being all nonchalant was kind of pissing me off. She was the most consistent shorty I'd had in a minute and it seemed like she ain't appreciate that shit. Just cause I ain't want to be out here lovesick and shit like Ju ain't mean that I was willing to let her fuck nobody else. That might have seemed selfish, I could admit that, but it was what it was.

"You so full of shit Troy," she chuckled and took her phone out my hand.

"So, you tryna say we not together?"

"Nope, we good how we are." She shrugged. "We can still fuck around and still do us when we feel like it."

I was stuck, shit; what was I supposed to say to some shit like that? Shorty was out here on some nigga shit and I couldn't say that I was happy about it, honestly, I didn't know how I felt. On one hand, it was the perfect set up. I could do what I wanted and still have her in a way, but I wasn't tryna share her lil ass either. Little did she know, I would agree to this shit, but it wasn't going down how she thought it was.

"Bet, now come here." I nodded and licked my lips. I'd been thinking about touching her since she walked in and I was trying to squeeze on her ass a little bit before Ju came back in.

"Aht, aht, not today, I gotta date. I was only bringing Niv up here to see Ju." She knocked my hand away with a smirk and then stood to her feet. I caught up to her just as she placed her hand on the doorknob and pressed my body into hers.

"That's all you came for? You know you wanted me to see you in these lil ass shorts," I grunted in her ear as I untied her drawstring so that I could get reacquainted with her pussy real quick.

"Yesssss, that's all I came for," she managed to get out as I slowly grazed her clit.

"Oh, you wanna lie and shit huh? Lock that door right quick."

"What! Hell no, I told you I got a date Troy," she whined and tried to wiggle away, but I had her pinned.

"I know, I'm bouta send you with somethin to remember me by." I smirked cockily at the moan that she let slip out after I said that. If her wetness wasn't a giveaway that she was feigning for the dick, then her moans of pleasure while I continued to stroke her clit damn sure was.

With one hand still deep inside her shorts, I used the other to lock the door and then released myself from the basketball shorts I wore. By now, Niyah was so into it that she was helping me by shimmying out of her own clothes, and I didn't even hesitate to slip my dick inside of her. The fact that I'd just went in her raw wasn't even on my mind when I felt her velvety walls.

"God damn Niyah baby." I paused and just sat in the pussy, unable to move without shooting a baby off in her.

Once I got my nut under control, I held her tightly around the waist and slowly moved my way in and out of her pussy. She bent down further without prompting, creating the perfect arch in her back as she let out a sexy ass whimper.

"Oooh, mmm." I cupped her breast as I dug deeper. No lie, Niyah had the kind of pussy that would have a nigga stuck. I was already thinking of ways to ruin her date and get her back to my crib. It wasn't no way another nigga was about to get a chance to slide up in shorty. I just wasn't bouta let that happen.

I placed one last kiss on her neck, then spun her around so that we were facing each other. I had to switch shit up because I could feel myself about to splash off again already. The look of pleasure on her face let me know that she was seconds away from cumming herself and I had to taste it. I kissed my way down her body and helped her completely out of her shorts, before propping her leg over my shoulder and diving into her pussy face first.

"Oh shiiiit Troy!" She shuddered at my tongue slipping between her folds and then held onto my head. I wasn't a pussy eating nigga, but I was trying to slurp up every last juice Niyah had to give. Her pussy definitely tasted as good as it felt. "Eat that shit zaddy!"

I must have been doing that shit right because she started bucking hard as hell before her body finally went limp, but I wasn't done with shorty yet. Standing to my feet, I wiped my mouth and grinned widely.

"I'm zaddy huh?"

"Hell yeah!" she said breathlessly and pulled me in for a kiss. I tongued shorty down and lifted each of her legs into the crooks of my arms, gaining a squeal out of her. Almost like it was meant for her pussy, my dick slid right in with no guidance.

"Mmph, this pussy so fuckin good Niyah, shit!" I grunted against her lips as I slammed into her over and over. She was working them muscles on me and, despite how hard I was trying to hold back, I could feel myself about to come.

Boom! Boom! Boom!

"Nigga, I know y'all asses ain't in there fuckin!" Ju banged on the door and yelled, just as Niyah squeezed the last bit of nut out of me. I slowly let her legs down as we both panted heavily.

"Niyah, you so nasty, bitch! I'm tellin yo mama!" Nivea said next.

"Mind yo business bitch!" Niyah's voice came out shaky and breathless.

"Come on before they kick down the door ma," I joked while laughing.

"Nigga, I can't feel my fuckin legs, hell. I need a minute!"

I ain't wanna tell her, but that's exactly the effect I was going for. She finally got herself together enough to push herself away from the door and pull some feminine wipes up out her bag. I started to make a big deal about her carrying that shit around when we hadn't spoken in a week, but I let the shit ride cause I was gone make sure her ass ain't use them with no other nigga. By the time we finished getting redressed, Ju and Nivea was gone and I was low key pissed that they had did all that at the door just to dip out. I even tried to get Niyah little short ass to get in another round, but she was still talking about going on that damn date. She skipped her ass out of there with a smirk, but I knew it wasn't gone be no date cause she was gone be in my bed before the night was over.

CHAPTER 12

Savage

I felt like a straight up sucka for being so quick to jump to Nivea's aid, but wasn't no nigga gone be putting his hands on her. When I saw the bruises around her neck, it took everything in my power not to go straight to her crib and air that bitch out. She told me that she had left right after he choked her though, and the first place she thought to go was to my O.G. She was the one who had convinced Nivea to try and call me. The part of me that was still hurt from her betrayal stopped me from answering every time, and now I was regretting that shit.

I stole glances at her as I drove her back to her mama crib, unable to deny how much I missed her and the kids. The last week had been a busy one for me and Troy, so it had been easy not to think about them, but now with Nivea in my presence it was hard to ignore her scent, hard not to get back in sync with her breathing, her heartbeat. And hard not to want to touch her. Yeah, I was a straight up sucka.

I tried to think of ways to open up a conversation between the two of us so that the ride wouldn't be so tense, but I kept coming up with a blank. Despite her coming to me about the Quad situation, we were still stuck on two things. The fact that she left me for that nigga, (which she claims she didn't) and the fact that she'd done it because she thought I killed that nigga's mama and brother. Even though I'd actually done it, I wanted her to have more faith in me, or at least wait to talk to me and be her own judge of my guilt. That whole thing had me questioning whether or not she fucked with me like I fucked with her. Hell, it really wasn't a question at this point.

Pulling into the driveway at her O.G.'s crib was bittersweet, I wasn't ready to leave her, but at the same time the strong ass feelings I was having being so close was fucking with me. Nivea brought out a side of me that was obviously too soft for the task at hand, and I needed to stay in Savage mode.

"You gone come look at the truck for me?" she asked after we'd been sitting there for a second. Without meaning to, I frowned.

"Fuck you and them bad ass kids do to a 2018 already!?" I was only half joking. Nivea's face matched mine, like she had a reason to be irritated when she'd just messed up something that was brand new! And that I had paid for!

"First of all, we ain't do nothin to it! It was runnin just fine the other day, I don't know what's wrong with it."

"Come on man," I said, reaching for the door handle. Nivea knew damn well I ain't know shit about cars, but I figured it was just a ploy for me to stay longer, and regardless of my doubts, I was willing to play along. I stepped out of the car, feigning an attitude with Nivea right behind me. "Where the keys at?"

She silently dug around in her purse until she came out with them and placed them in my outstretched hand. She'd barely let them go before I closed my fingers and started towards her truck. I could sense the attitude radiating off of her, but my feelings right now were all messed up. Granted, I loved Nivea and I was definitely at that nigga Quad's head for putting his hands on her but, if she wouldn't have had doubts about my innocence, none of that shit would have happened. I was more than confused about how to handle things with her and it was irritating the fuck out of me.

Hitting the unlock button on her key fob, I let myself into the truck and tried to start it a few times. It wasn't making any damn noise at all, not clicking or nothing the shit was dead silent. Nivea came and stood in the open doorway and gave me a look like "I told you so", while I tried to turn it over again. I popped the hood and went to take a look at the engine, even though the shit was foreign to me.

"Oh shit, Ju Savage out here! Let me call you back bitch!" My head was down trying to look like I knew what I was doing, so I didn't see her, but I definitely heard Nivea's loud ass sister coming. She must have ran over because before I could even lift my head, I could see the lower half of her body standing on the side of the truck.

I took my time coming out from under the hood because I wasn't really trying to deal with Nivea's rachet ass sister. On the few occasions that I'd come in contact with her, she had been extra as hell and everybody knew I didn't like that shit. I peeped Nivea rolling her eyes, before she crossed her arms over her chest and gave me her attention.

"Heeeeey Ju!" she said excitedly, throwing her arms up like she was about to give me a hug, but I put a stop to that with a whole palm to her face. She stepped back with a laugh, knowing not to try and knock my hand away and pulled a compact from her pocket.

"Sup Nadia," I grunted, wiping my hands off on my jeans, and frowning at the stain her makeup had left on them.

"Ju, you play too much; now, I gotta fix my makeup," she giggled, patting at her lips with her index finger.

"You need to wipe all that messy shit off, and yo ass payin for my pants to be dry cleaned too." The look of stupidity on her face would have made me laugh under different circumstances, but I was dead ass serious about my jeans. She waved me off, still laughing like an airhead and I was about to let her know I wasn't playing with her ass, but Nivea cut me off.

"Could you tell what was wrong with the truck?"

"Hell naw, I don't know what's goin on wit yo shit." I told her with a shrug. "I'll get it towed today tho-"

"Damnnnnn Niv! I'm tryna be like you when I grow up, you got two niggas jumpin through hoops for yo ass!" Nadia's stupid ass said, reaching out to give Nivea a high five. Nivea looked shocked and embarrassed, and I couldn't help but narrow my eyes at her. If it wasn't for her jumping ship as soon as I got locked up, then she wouldn't have shit to be embarrassed about.

"Aye, get yo peoples man," I advised, not wanting to be the reason that her sister got her feelings hurt.

"Why would you say some goofy ass shit like that Nadia? You so fuckin extra! Take yo shit startin ass in the house!" Nivea finally hissed as she shot daggers her sister's way. If the shit her sister had just said hadn't put me in a bad mood, then I was sure my face would've shown my approval of her checking Nadia's ass. I had definitely rubbed off on her in a good way because it seemed like she was standing up for herself more and more.

"What? I ain't even say shit, I'm just statin facts." Nadia feigned confusion, but I was sure that her ass knew exactly what she was doing when she said that shit, and she'd gotten the desired effect out of me cause I was irritated as fuck.

"Bye Nadia!" Niv spoke stiffly with her fists balled up at her sides.

"Girl, don't be mad at me cause yo ass out here flip floppin between niggas. I swear, you get on my nerves." Nadia huffed and stomped her way into the house. As soon as she was out of eyesight, Nivea let out a deep breath.

"Sorry about that... now, what was you sayin?" she tried to continue with our conversation like her sister hadn't just come and put her business out. I started not to even say shit to her and let her figure out what to do about the truck on her own, but I couldn't even be petty to her, no matter how bad I thought she deserved it.

"I'ma send a tow over for you, but let me get up outta here quick. I got some shit to do," I lied and handed her the keys back as I walked past, not even waiting on her to say shit. I ignored her calling out to me and got in my car, ready to put distance between us real fast. If Nivea's betrayal hadn't been on my mind before, it for damn sure was now.

That whole scene back there had put me on edge. I already felt like I was a sucka, to see that other people was thinking the same way had me mad as hell. Usually when I needed to figure some shit out, I went to Troy, but that nigga had already showed me who side he was on when he urged me to talk to her at the studio. It was clear that he was on whatever side that Niyah was, so I needed to talk to somebody that wasn't so close to the situation. And the first person who came to mind was Pree.

I knew his old ass was at the studio, so I decided to slide through. The parking lot looked a lot more crowded than it usually did. He'd told me that he had been getting a lot of business since me Troy and I had cut our deal, and I was happy to see that the move had benefited him too.

I parked in the first empty spot I saw and made my way inside, surprised to see Pree's office door closed. That ain't stop me from twisting the knob and walking right in. I damn near ran right back out at the sight of my O.G. in there sitting on that nigga's lap and giggling while he whispered in her ear. As soon as she saw that it was me who had walked in, she hopped up fast as hell, almost falling. Pree helped steady her and then looked my way with a frown.

"Damn, you don't knock when you see a closed door nigga?" he fumed.

"Not when it's my dad's closed door. If I had known y'all was up in here boo'd up, I most definitely would have tho." It was weird as fuck seeing my mama caking with a nigga and even weirder that the nigga was Pree's old ass. I really hadn't even seen much, but the little bit that I did see had my stomach damn near turning.

"Hey, Judah baby, you got a chance to talk to Nivea yet?" my mama questioned, coming over to where I stood with her lips poked out to kiss me. I dodged her ass quick as hell and gave her a dry ass hug instead.

"You ain't bouta put them lips on me after you and Pree been up in here with the door closed."

"Boy, you came up out my stomach! I can kiss you whenever I want to!" She smacked me upside the head and proceeded to plant a kiss on my cheek that I wiped clean off as soon as she turned to Pree with a satisfied grin. "Now, speakin of kisses, did you and Nivea kiss and make up?"

"Mann, I ain't messin with shorty like that, her ass too flaky for me," I lied, garnering a nasty look from her.

"Says the nigga that was a drunk, cryin fool, over her just a week ago."

"Mannnn, wasn't nobody cryin over her ass! Pree, get yo baby mama man."

"You can't tell nobody to get me-"

"Aye Jack, let me talk to him right quick. I'm gone be home in a minute anyway," Pree spoke up from his spot across the room, and I was shocked to see her not put up a fight and even more surprised that he referred to her crib as home. I guess they were making shit official these days.

"Fine! But don't think you handled me just now. I'm only goin cuz I gotta start dinner for my baby anyway," she grumbled irritably, grabbing her purse from the file cabinet it sat on.

"Woman, you already know I can handle you," Pree got up and said as he wrapped his arms around her. This nigga got to whispering in her ear and shit, and whatever he was saying had her old ass grinning and blushing hard as hell. My lip curled in disgust at them being over affectionate and shit while I was standing there. It was one thing to know that your parents fucked around like that, but it was a whole nother thing to see that shit.

"Aye man, cut all that nasty shit out." I fumed with my face balled up.

"You just mad cause you can't do it, with yo stubborn ass!" My mama waved me off with a roll of her eyes, before giving Pree one last kiss and sashaying out the room.

"Damn young, yo mama still bad as hell," he said, looking after her lustfully. Low key, I was happy that my O.G. was happy and, since I had a better understanding of what went down, I was cool with Pree being my dad. Still, I wasn't that comfortable with them being together that I was ready to see them kissing and shit! Hell naw!

"I ain't come here to hear all that!" I groaned, causing him to smirk. He walked back to his seat and leaned back with his hands folded in front of him.

"Ayite, what's up then?"

Now that it was time to finally express the reason I'd come, my ass didn't know how to get it out. I fell into the only other chair in the room and threw my head back as I released a heavy sigh.

"Mannnn, shorty got me all the way fucked up right now,"

I finally said after we had sat in silence for a minute or two while I got my thoughts together.

"You uh, wanna elaborate?"

"Ion't know shit. I fuck with Nivea. She the first female I ever said I love you to, outside of my O.G. and Janiah."

"Ayite, so what's the issue then?" he cut me off and asked.

"Shit, her ass left me for that clown ass nigga as soon as somebody told her some shit she ain't wanna hear about me!" Just saying the shit out loud had me heated. I didn't think that Nivea had tried to play me. I knew without a doubt that I had her ass on lock, and there was no way that she was gone leave me for that nigga. My biggest issue was feeling like she betrayed me. She had let dude goofy ass get away with shit for years but, the minute that she *heard* that I'd done some shit with no proof, she jumped ship quick as hell. Like damn, I couldn't even get the benefit of the doubt with her ass.

"So, you sayin you don't trust her?" Pree's face showed that he was trying to piece shit together.

"Hell naw! Who's to say her ass ain't gone dip on me the next time she hear some shit? I'm bouta be on some celebrity shit, and you know it's always some lies being spread when you famous. I ain't tryna set myself up for that again. Naw, I can't even go for that."

"Then, leave her alone, simple." He shrugged like it was really just that easy. Truth was, it had been easier to pull the trigger on Jay and his mama than it would ever be to leave Nivea alone for good. It wasn't something that I wanted to do, and I didn't even think I was capable of trying to.

"Naw, I ain't tryna do that either." I shook my head as I answered and Pree laughed.

"Well, that's yo answer then."

"Huh?" My eyebrows dipped in confusion. "What you mean that's my answer man?"

He let out a deep breath and shook his head like he pitied my slow ass. "Boy, if you love her despite yo issues, then that's reason enough to give it a second chance right there. Personally, I don't think that this incident is proof that she's not loyal. We both know she's green as fuck so, off top, she probably didn't want any parts of dealing with the possibility that you killed some people, especially some people she has ties to. I ain't sayin its right, but at least look at it from her point of view. That's what this love shit is all about, being aware of the other person's wants and needs and compromising. Now, if you can put yoself in her shoes and still not agree with how she went about things, then leave her alone but, if you can understand where she coming from and why, then give her another chance. Both of y'all seem miserable without each other, so y'all might as well make up so we can take care of that other thing. Your bail hearing is comin up soon," he added, giving me a cryptic look. It was true. Between the gigs and searching for them hoe ass niggas Quad and Keys, I'd barely remembered the bail hearing.

"You right, I'ma handle it tho," I promised, standing to my feet.

"Ayite, hit me up if you need somethin young." He came over and gave me a pound before I left out. Pree had given me a lot to think about. I would do what he had suggested but, ultimately, I knew that before I could fully jump back into shit with Nivea, her baby daddy had to die. And I was trying to make that happen as soon as possible.

CHAPTER 13

*S*aniyah
After fucking around with Troy, my damn legs were tired as hell, but that wasn't gone stop me from going on my date, if that's what he was thinking. Who was I kidding though? That nigga definitely thought he was about to cock block my date. You would think though that he would be willing to let me do me since he was obviously doing him, but niggas was crazy as hell. They expected you to just wait around until they got ready to settle down and be faithful. But, if that's what Troy thought was about to happen, then he was going to be highly disappointed.

When I left out of the studio, I was happy to see that Nivea and Savage had left together. I knew that telling him about Quad's bitch ass putting his hands on her would do the trick. His ass was lucky I wasn't there cause I would have tased the shit out of him. I couldn't wait until Troy and Savage caught up with him.

As soon as I pulled out of the parking lot, my phone was going off with text messages from Troy. I couldn't help the giggle of delight that slipped out cause he was doing exactly what I knew he would. Now, while I liked Troy and had wanted to see where things would go with him, I wasn't about to play his little adolescent games. Why should I? I was bad as fuck! Smooth caramel skin, with a cute face and body to match. He was a damn fool if he thought I was just gone wait around on him! Nope, but I could show him better than I could tell him and I was going to start with this date.

Brandon was one of the doctors who worked the emergency room on-call a couple times a week. I'd already had my eye on him being that he was the youngest doctor there, add to that the fact that he was well spoken, highly educated, and paid and I saw a match made in heaven. When he had approached me, he let me know that he had wanted to come at me for a while, and he'd finally gotten the nerve to ask me out. That was flattering and I quickly let him talk me into a date. I was an equal opportunity dater. I could date a rough ass hood nigga, but I could also date a suit and tie wearing nigga. Anyway, I threw my shades on and continued on my way home blasting that Cardi B, *I went through your phone.*

Once I got to my apartment, I slid out of my shoes and headed straight to the shower. I cut the water on the setting that I liked and stripped out of my clothes while I waited on the temperature to adjust. Grabbing up my 32-inch weave, I placed my bonnet on and stepped inside, letting the water run over my body for a minute before adding some Caress and a towel to the mix.

After handling my hygiene, I dried off and slipped on my pink terry cloth robe, since the a.c. in there was kicking and went to my couch to skim through social media. I had a few hours before my date and I wanted to see if Kisha's baby daddy had hit me back. Seeing that I didn't have not one message in my inbox from him and that he hadn't even been active in days had me frowning my face up. There was definitely something crazy going on and, if I had to call DCFS myself, I was going to get to the bottom of it. I made a mental note to check into it further, but a call from Brandon flashed across my screen and I hurried to answer it.

"Hey you," I purred, unable to hide the smile in my voice.

"Hey love, I was just calling to make sure we were still on for tonight." His voice was smooth as hell and I almost melted in my seat.

"Of course, I'm home about to start getting ready for you."

"Ahhh, and I thought I was the only one that was anxious for 7 to roll around," he chuckled.

"Nope, I'm more than ready to see what you have in store for us."

"Well, I'll see you soon love."

"And I'll be waiting." I cheesed as I disconnected the call. That calling me love shit was the sexiest thing I'd ever heard. Looking at the time, I saw that I had roughly three hours before he would get there, so I cut on Pandora and connected my phone to the Bluetooth speaker as I got ready for my date.

By a quarter to seven, I was dressed and ready to go in a pale pink bodycon dress, with nude red bottoms to match. I'd kept my jewelry simple, only donning a gold cross that nestled right in between my breasts, and my gold hoop earrings. It hadn't taken long to put some big Kim K curls in my hair, and I'd went full glam with my makeup.

I stood in the mirror primping and posting pictures on social media, when a knock on the door drew my attention to the clock. Brandon was a few minutes early, which gave him brownie points for sure. I loved a punctual man. After a last minute glance at myself, I put on a seductive smile and opened the door to see Troy standing there next to Brandon, who looked uncomfortable as hell.

"What the fuck do you think you doin Troy?" I hissed, glaring at him angrily while he just grinned.

"Fuck you mean, we had a date shorty. Ain't that what you said earlier after we fuck-"

"I said *I* had a date nigga!" I hurried to cut him off and snuck a glance at Brandon to make sure he hadn't heard him.

"Uhh... is this a bad time Saniyah?" Brandon asked with his brow dipped in concern.

"Actually, it is my nigga; we had a date already set up. Plus, I already done beat her pussy out the frame earlier, so it really ain't no need for you to be here. I'm gone tell you the truth, you don't wanna take her nowhere tonight; she bout gone be havin flash backs and shit, then I'ma have to come pick her up cuz I know you ain't gone be able to help!"

I couldn't do shit but rub my damn temple as this nigga singlehandedly ran off my date. His ass was talking so crazy that I cut out of the conversation after that! I could barely force myself to look at Brandon, but I did and the look on his face was that of an old ass rich white man. His shit was red, and I could tell that he was embarrassed and angry, but he knew better than to try to voice that shit.

"Brandon, I'm so sor-" I started, but he held up a hand to stop me.

"Save it, I knew better than to try and date a black bitch!" he scoffed and attempted to walk away.

"Excuse you!" I grabbed the arm of his suit, trying to snatch his ass back, but Troy's dumb ass grabbed me up into a bear hug. "I got yo bitch! Bitch!" I struggled against him, ready to use my new can of mace on dude.

"Aye, calm yo lil ass down man, I got this!" Troy gritted in my face and sat me down inside of my doorway, before he turned around and hit Brandon, who was still standing there, with a two piece I know he ain't see coming. My mouth dropped open as he hit the ground and covered his face with his hands.

"Troy! What the hell?" I went to try to help Brandon up, but Troy quickly grabbed my arm.

"Girl, I wish you would help dude hoe ass up! Get the fuck in the house man!" he ordered. As bad as I wanted to argue, the look in his eye stopped me and I stepped right over Brandon's body and stomped inside, making sure to slam the door behind me.

"This nigga got me so fucked up!" I grumbled, pacing my small living room in anger. Not even a minute later, Troy walked in tucking his gun in his waist. When he noticed me glaring his way, he grinned widely. "Don't smile at me! I told yo ass I had a date!"

He was pissing me off acting as if he had a right to interfere with my love life. Especially, since he seemed to not want to be involved in it unless we were fucking or I was giving my attention to another man. And I was mad at myself for noticing how fucking good he was looking right then. He had changed his clothes since earlier at the studio and was now rocking a navy blue Givenchy, button up, with sand brown straight leg jeans and some "navy gum" Jordan 11's. Damn, he always made the most simple shit look sexy!

"With that lame ass nigga? You know he wasn't gone be able to handle you, he couldn't even say yo name right! *Is this a bad time Saniyah?*" he mocked as he swaggered over and pulled me into his arms. Even though I tried to resist, I couldn't stop myself from laughing at his impression of Brandon.

"That shit not funny Troy! I was lookin forward to goin out," I lied. The shit was hilarious and I didn't mind him running Brandon's bitch ass off. There was no way I was tryna date a nigga that said shit like that to a female, instead of addressing the male that was in his face.

"That's what I'm here for, I'll take you anywhere you wanna go."

I squinted my eyes at him, unsure of if I believed him or not. He'd fuck around and be on his damn phone the whole night. I shook my head emphatically. Troy was in rare form tonight and I ain't know if I wanted to subject myself to anymore embarrassment.

"No, I'm tryna go somewhere that you have to make reservations, not no damn Red Lobster."

"Dammmnn, Red Lobster don't got reservations?" he asked wide eyed, like he was shocked to hear it. I rolled my eyes and went to walk away, but he snatched me back by my waist. "Ayite, ayite. I'm just fuckin with you girl, come on."

"You so full of shit Troy, I'm goin to bed," I huffed while pouting. It felt like he was taking me for a joke.

"Nah, for real, I'm tryna take you somewhere nice; you lookin too muthafuckin good in that dress to just go take it off." He looked me up and down in appreciation and licked his lips. After studying his face through squinted eyes, I slowly agreed with a nod, not bothering to mention how it would've been his fault if my dress did go to waste.

"Okay fine, you lucky I'm hungry," I finally sneered, causing him to chuckle. I was sure he was real satisfied with himself having ruined my date, but little did he know I wasn't going to allow him to have his cake and eat it too. Next time, I'd make sure not to run my mouth and have him fucking up my shit.

CHAPTER 14

*N*ivea
"Um Ms. Hynes, I'd like it if you joined us in the discussion."

I lifted my eyes to see that everyone had broken up into groups, and I was the only one still sitting in my own desk. My cheeks flamed in embarrassment as twenty pairs of eyes landed on me.

"Sorry Mr. Stone," I mumbled, gathering my notebook and pen so that I could join a group. Usually, I loved my English literature class and was always heavily involved in the lecture but, today, my mind was jumbled with thoughts of Judah.

It had been almost a week since that day he'd come over to look at the truck for me and I hadn't seen or heard from him since. Although he had kept his word and sent a tow truck over later that day, Nadia's slick ass comments had obviously pissed him off and that's why he was being so distant after I thought that we were getting along. Every day that I hadn't heard from him since had put me more and more into a funk. And it wasn't like I could just forget about him because the bigger he got, the more I heard his name and his music. Almost every day, some little groupie was approaching me and asking questions about him since the last they knew, we were together.

"Aye Nivea!" At the sound of my name, I stopped looking around for a group to join and saw this guy named Damien waving me over. I sighed inwardly because he was annoying as hell and the last person that I wanted to be in a group with. Me and him happened to be the oldest people in the class and he always attempted to try and get close to me because of it. Him and two girls named Mariah and Bianca had pushed the desks that they were in together. I was honestly surprised that he had gotten in a group with them cause they were notoriously rachet and, as soon as I joined them, the bullshit started.

"Thanks," I said through a tight lipped smile.

"No problem, we're just supposed to be answering the questions on the board. Nothin too hard." He shrugged. "Now, the first question-"

"Nah, fuck all that. Are you really the Nivea that goes with Ju Savage?" Mariah cut him off and asked. They both were leaned over the desk towards me with their brows raised in suspense. I stopped copying down the sentences and nodded, even though me and Judah were barely on speaking terms. I wasn't about to tell them bitches that.

"I knew that was yo ass!" Bianca said loudly, damn near jumping out of her seat. "How it feel to date a celebrity? Did you have to beat Kisha ass for that bullshit she pulled? No, wait! Is the sex good? I'm already knowing it is." She shot off question after question and I looked around, hoping that nobody else heard her dumb ass.

"Nah, the real question is why the fuck you in school if yo nigga gettin money like Savage?" Mariah asked and they both looked at me, really expecting an answer to that stupid shit.

Before I could even check them though, Damien gawked at me with wide eyes and said.

"You're in a relationship with somebody that calls himself Ju Savage? He must be a rapper?" The disapproval on his face showed how unhappy he was to hear that information, even though it wasn't none of his business.

"Hell yeah! He the shit too! I'm surprised he tryna settle down as young as he is though," Bianca inserted, giving me a sly look.

"Young?" Damien's frown deepened.

"Yeah, he bouta be 22." This drew his judgmental gaze my way, and I tried unsuccessfully to control the anger I felt about what he might have been thinking.

"So, he's twenty one?" It was a statement and a question at the same time, like he needed clarification of what he'd just been told. Mariah looked at him like he was slow and rolled her eyes.

"That's what she just said, ain't it?"

"Do you have a problem with his age Damien?" I dropped the pen I'd been holding and folded my hands together on top of the desk, waiting to see what bull shit came out of his mouth. He seemed alarmed that I asked and his eyes bucked at my forwardness.

"I guess not, I just didn't think you were the type to date one of these little gang banging rappers. I mean at your age and with four young children, a 'bad boy' is hardly what you should be attracted to." My mouth dropped open at the audacity of him to even feel as if that was appropriate to say to someone, especially someone that he didn't know outside of one class.

"First of all, I'm grown enough to make mature decisions about who I date and bring around my kids, and I'm also grown enough to not stereotype somebody I don't know simply because they're fuckin somebody that I wished I could! But, I ain't so grown that I won't call him up here to beat yo ass!" I spat, leaving him speechless.

"I know that's right!"

"And you!" I turned to Bianca, instantly wiping the look of appreciation off her face. "The next time you fix those crusty lips to ask me about how my man fucks me, I'm gone snatch them bitches off!"

Before she could even figure out how to respond, I was snatching up my stuff and storming towards the door. I ignored the teacher calling my name and didn't stop until I was outside of the building and searching for my car.

It took me all of five minutes to realize that my car was still in the shop. I'd driven my mama's little Maxima and had parked it in my usual spot, not thinking that I wouldn't recognize it when I got out of school. Taking a deep breath, I got in and pulled out my phone, disappointed that there wasn't any missed calls from Judah. I was conflicted on whether or not I should just give him a call, but he'd already been ignoring me and the only reason he'd even talked to me the last time was because of the incident with Quad. If I was being honest, I knew that this all was a direct result of how I'd reacted when he was arrested. Maybe I should have just waited on an explanation from him myself, but it was done now and I couldn't take it back. I really wished that I could though.

My phone vibrated in my hand, jolting me out my thoughts and I hurried to answer, only to see that it was Niyah calling. I connected it to the aux cord and pulled off as her voice filled the car.

"Heeeey bitch!" She came through loud as hell and I couldn't help but to laugh.

"Hey Niyah."

"Ugh, you sound dry as hell! Let me find out you in yo

feels cause Savage on that bullshit." I could tell that she was rolling her eyes, but what could I say? It was true.

"Welllll, everybody's man ain't comin through shuttin shit down," I teased. She'd told me about how Troy had fucked up her date and then took her out afterwards. I thought it was cute and funny as hell, but Niyah wasn't feeling it.

"Girl, fuck Troy! If he think this shit over, he got a rude ass awakening comin!" she huffed and started grumbling under her breath.

"Yeah okay, you saw what he did last time. He is not bouta let you date nobody else."

"I wanna see him stop me! That's why I'm callin you now, it's Friday biiitch! You know you wanna go out with me!" I immediately started shaking my head no.

"Hell no! You ain't bouta have Troy yankin me out nobody club! No!" I shook my head again like she could see me.

"You a scary ass hoe! Troy and Savage got a show tonight, they not even gone be in the vicinity of no damn club. Trust me." I mulled over the idea in my head, trying to weigh the pros and cons of going out with her. The fact that the guys would be busy definitely put me at ease but, at the same time, there was a possibility of running into Quad. I hadn't seen him since the day that his crazy ass had choked me out, and I didn't want to even think about what he would do if I ran into him again. Even though it didn't look like he had been back to the apartment every time I stopped through for clothes, I still wasn't comfortable staying there. I figured though that the chances of seeing him out would be slim to none, considering that he was a witness in the case against Judah. That and the fact that I'd just stormed out of my last class of the day made me agree to go with her.

"Ayite, but *only* because Judah and this shit at school got me needing a drink!" I admitted.

"Hold up, what happened at school?" she wanted to know, and I quickly filled her in on what had just happened, getting mad all over again just talking about it.

"Oh, hell naw! You shoulda slapped all three of they asses! They had you fucked up best friend!" I laughed as she went off, not giving me a chance to say nothing.

"Are you done or is you finished?"

"Bitch, fuck you! I'm bouta look for a new bestie cause you be trippin! I'm out here defending you and cursin all in this store, but you wanna play! That's why you ain't even say that shit right!"

"Okay, I'm sorry bestie. What time you wanna leave tonight?"

"Be ready by eleven heffa and don't make me have to come in yo mama house actin a fool cuz you ain't ready neither!" she fussed.

"Girl, bye!"

"Bye!"

The phone beeped, letting me know that she'd finally hung up and "destroyed" by TXS blasted through the car since that was the last song I'd been listening to before I went into school. A few minutes later, I was pulling into my mama's driveway behind a truck that was almost identical to the one Judah bought me aside from the color. I got out and inspected the silver beauty curiously before going inside.

"Ma, Ju was here and he gave me some money!" Quiana jumped up from where she was sitting on the couch, flashing a hundred dollar bill in my face. I snatched it away to get a better look and I'd be damned if that nigga hadn't really gave her a hundred damn dollars.

"When was he here?" I needed to know. I guess I should have been happy that he still wanted to have some type of a relationship with the kids at least, but I still felt slighted. The least he could have done was come over when I was home.

"He came right after you left for school, and he brought you another car too! He said don't break it," she continued, unaware of the mood she was putting me in. It was just like him to bring his ass over after I left, like he wanted to avoid me! He was really doing too much and it was starting to make me dislike his ignorant ass. I should have been happy that he had replaced the truck for me, even though he didn't have to, but I just couldn't get over how he went about it. I hurried to dial his ass up, fully prepared to leave him a long nasty voicemail and was rendered speechless when he actually answered.

"Wassup Niv?" he said, sounding like he was expecting a call from me, and everything that I'd been ready to say got stuck in my throat. I waved Quiana away, since she was still standing right in my face, trying to be nosy as I got my thoughts together. She went back to her spot on the couch, but I still stepped out onto the front porch for a little more privacy. "Hello?"

"Yeah, I'm here."

"Well, say something man, I'm tryna get ready for this show tonight." My neck snapped at his tone, and I gasped.

"You don't gotta sound so irritated, I was just wondering how long I gotta drive this truck before mine is fixed?" The lie rolled right off my tongue like I'd planned it.

"Yo truck ain't gettin fixed shorty, somebody put some shit in yo gas tank that fucked up the engine."

"What the hell! Somebody did what!" I fumed, wondering who in the fuck would mess with my car.

"That don't even matter, you got a new one with a lock on the tank so don't even trip." He was being extremely cool about it, like aside from replacing my truck he had everything under control. I couldn't help but feel like he knew who had did that shit and just didn't wanna tell me.

"Did Kisha do this shit Judah!"

"Nigga, we ain't seen Kisha in months Niv, you trippin! Yo bitch ass baby daddy more likely to have done it than Kisha!" he snapped. "Look, man, you got a new car, let me worry about all that other shit." He cut me off before I could say anything else and then hung up. Shocked, I pulled the phone away from my ear to look at the screen and make sure he'd really hung up on me. Judah was acting real funky with me and I really didn't know how to take it.

Pissed, I stomped back into the house, ignoring the look Quiana was giving me, and headed straight to the kitchen where my mother was sitting at the table looking through a magazine.

"Hey ma," I sighed, grabbing a bottle of water from the fridge and cracking it open right there.

"Hey lil girl, what got you lookin so tense in the face?" she read me quickly without me even saying anything.

"I just had a long day is all, I'll be fine." I didn't want to further trouble her with my petty bullshit; I had already moved into her space with the kids. She hadn't complained or given me any indication that she was ready for us to go, but I still couldn't help feeling like a burden at times. I really needed to figure out what I was going to do as far as taking my ass home or finding somewhere else to live.

"Mmmhmm," she hummed in that tone that only a mother could give. "That sound like a lie girl, either you havin issues with the new one or you havin issues with the old one. I already know what you got goin on with that old one, so it must be bout Judah."

"Yeah, it's Judah's petty ass." I finally grumbled in anger and rolled my eyes. My mama looked at me with a stale face and returned to reading her magazine. It took me a full minute to realize that she wasn't about to say anything. "Ma?"

"What?"

"You just gone leave me hangin?" I questioned, completely confused by her attitude. She let out a deep sigh and turned her attention to me.

"I try not to tell you I told you so, but I told yo ass about that nigga Quad. Now, he's come back and fucked up what you got goin on with Judah-"

"No, Judah messed us up by being involved in those murders!" I jumped in, causing her to buck her eyes at me.

"First of all, you gone lower your fuckin tone. Secondly, did you get told or shown proof of this because that's two different things?" She tilted her head, waiting on me to answer.

"Welllll, the warrant for his arrest pretty much did both," I trailed stupidly.

"Nivea, you can't be this dumb girl. You know CPD ain't got no problem lockin niggas up for shit but, regardless of that, you still want him despite feelin that he did it sooooo what is your point?"

I stood there, silently unable to give her an answer. *What was my point?* I was torn between believing in Judah's word and the word of numerous people, the main one being Quad. I didn't want to be the type of female that believed everything my man told me to my detriment, but I also didn't want to lose Judah, only to find out that he had been innocent. Nobody had ever loved me as good as he did, not even Quad and, unfortunately, I had always thought that Quad's love was the ultimate until meeting Judah. It was crazy that in such a short amount of time he came in and showed me what unconditional love looked and felt like.

Now, he basically was acting like he didn't want anything to do with me, and I didn't know how to take that. I guess I could understand his reasoning, especially considering his lifestyle, but that didn't make it any easier to accept.

"Well, it don't matter how much I may want him cause he not fuckin with me right now anyway," I admitted bitterly.

"Girl, can you blame him? I told yo ass not to be fuckin back around with Quad! Now, he's caused a rift between you and Judah, but just because he's not fuckin with you how you want him to don't mean he completely gone." She shrugged, and I rolled my eyes.

"His ass sure ignoring me, and when he do talk to me it's like he's too irritated to talk."

"That don't mean nothin'; he's a man, so he's gotta do something to save face but, if he didn't fuck with you, would he have brought yo ass a new truck? I'll answer for you, hell naw! That wasn't something he did out of the kindness of his heart; he replaced that truck because he loves you, he loves those kids, and he knows that y'all need to get around. Now, he may need some time and you most definitely have to prove yourself trustworthy to him, but I'm sure that he has intentions on getting back with you. The question is will you be able to accept that blessin?" She raised her brow ominously and picked up her glass and magazine, leaving me alone in my thoughts.

What she'd said made a lot of sense, but I couldn't help worrying that while Judah was on this whole "punish Nivea" trip, that he may entertain himself with another Kisha, if not the goofy hoe herself. Aside from begging, I wasn't sure how to get back in his good graces, but I would just enlist Niyah's help with that as soon as possible because I was tired of being without my man.

CHAPTER 15

*Q*uad
    I hadn't been back to the house since the day I'd put my hands on Nivea, meaning I hadn't seen her or my kids in weeks. I wasn't too pressed about seeing Nivea; honestly, I could go without having to see her. For one, I was ashamed of choking her the way I had and, for two, I wasn't blind to the way she'd switched up on a nigga. Right now, I didn't know what I wanted to do about her; we had years in, and I had her groomed just how I wanted her until that little nigga Savage came along. He definitely needed to go whether it was behind bars or a pine box; I needed to get him out the picture asap. And since the police were dragging their damn feet locking his ass up, I'd take the pine box for 300.

"Baby, put that away and come lay back down," Desiree whined, coming up behind me where I sat at the foot of her bed and wrapping her arms around my neck. I quickly shrugged her off and continued loading up my gun.

"Didn't I tell you to stop all that whinin and shit man damn!" She was really starting to be a pain in the ass. If she wasn't hounding me about testifying, then she was all over me trying to cuddle and shit. This shit wasn't supposed to go on past the prison walls but, somehow, she'd managed to wiggle her way into my real life and I was more than tired of her.

"I wasn't whining; I just want some of your attention! If yo ass ain't out running the streets, then you're here with yo nose stuck in that phone or the game! You never have time for me since you been home! It's like you don't wanna be with me now!"

I didn't need to turn around to know that she was back there crying like a damn idiot. Could you tell why I was annoyed? Her ass was delusional as fuck to think that we were about to turn a relationship of convenience into something more. She had a whole husband and a kid out here! Plus, she was more than ten years older than me, and she worked with law enforcement! Why would a nigga like me ever consider something serious with her? I put the last bullet in the chamber and snapped my gun closed, before standing to my feet and turning to face her.

"You already know what I'm on out here, y'all ain't really tryna lock that nigga up! And as long as he out, I gotta be worried bout him doin the same shit to me that he did to my brother and my mama! For a married bitch with a job, you got way too much time on yo hands to be clockin me like that!" I fumed, disgusted at the sight of her sitting on the bed with a face full of tears.

"I left Rick, okay! I left him to be with you!"

"Why the fuck would you do some stupid shit like that D? Damn!" She knew that I had a whole bitch before we even started fucking around and now just because we wasn't talking, her ass thought it was ok to leave her damn husband.

"I did it because I love you and… because I'm pregnant." She finally said and, if I was close enough, I would've choked the shit out of her. I'd only been up in her ass raw a handful of times, and each time I made her ass eat a morning after pill. My eyes narrowed as I took her in, wondering if she was conniving enough to trap a nigga.

"You know I wasn't tryna have a baby with you, man, what the fuck was you thinkin?" I paced the small bedroom pinching the bridge of my nose. I needed to calm the fuck down before I beat that baby out of her and landed my ass right back in prison.

"I'm thinkin that obviously our baby is meant to live because despite the plan b, I'm still pregnant. I ain't think you would be excited, but damn you don't have to be such a dick!"

"Do you fuckin hear yo self? You're married!" I stressed.

"So! You sholl keep bringin up my husband now since I'm pregnant, but yo ass wasn't thinkin bout him when we was makin this baby Quad!" She'd gone from crying to screaming, and I ain't have time to be going back and forth with her. I needed to head out and take care of this business before it was too late.

"Look, all that shit is irrelevant, get rid of it and go back to yo husband," I told her with finality, before grabbing up my snapback and leaving the room. I ignored her screaming my name on that dramatic shit.

She didn't even understand that the last thing I needed before I set out to kill Savage was her ass in my ear talking about another problem I would have to take care of. If she thought for one second that she was keeping that baby and we would be living out some twisted fantasy of a family, then she was dumber than I thought.

I spent half the ride to the club still stuck on what D was talking about, and the other half going over what I would do when I was in Savage's presence. When I finally pulled onto the block that club Ki$$ was on, I could see that the line was down the street and around the corner. Security was out the ass too and I knew it was because Savage and Troy was going to be in the building. Troy had posted on their Instagram where they would be, so it seemed like half the city had come out. I looked at the circus that was going on out there and shook my head as I drove past. There was no way that I was getting in with my gun tonight, not with security beefed up for them niggas to make an appearance.

I hit the block a couple of times looking for a parking spot and lucked up on one a couple buildings down. In that amount of time, the line had barely moved and I didn't even think that Savage and Troy had made it there yet. I got comfortable in my seat and pulled up the fake Instagram page I'd made so that I could follow Troy, since he was the one that posted his every move and, sure enough, there was a live of him in a limo on the way. The sight of Savage sitting in the cut with a bottle had me pissed. I couldn't stand that little nigga and it went way past him killing my family. If I was being real with myself, he'd done me a favor because both my mama and brother were fucked up and I only leaned on them when I was locked up. Shit, a lot of people didn't even know that I had a brother because his dumb ass stayed in some shit. That's what I liked to believe anyway, but it was my ties to the police that had him not really fucking with me, but I ain't give a fuck. That nigga had his ways about himself too, but I wasn't gone speak on it right now. The only reason I'd made such a big deal about it to Nivea was because I thought that it would make her believing me easier, but we all see how that shit played out. I watched the live until he cut it off since they were about to pull up to the club, and got my guns ready. I planned on ending this shit tonight.

CHAPTER 16

*S*avage

I wasn't excited about going to this damn club, not even a little bit but, since the show had went well, Troy convinced me to show my face. The plan was to only be there for an hour or so and then go home. Not only was I tired, but the fact that I had yet to find a for sure location on Keys or Quad had me in a bad mood. Add to that the shit that I was going through with Nivea and a nigga just wasn't in the mood for shit.

"Nigga, pick yo fuckin face up! Our show was just lit as fuck and you over there lookin all pissed," Troy said, giving me a light shove and handing the blunt he was smoking over. His ass had been amped up since we'd left the show and had went live a few times already trying to get the city out to club Ki$$ to party with us.

"I'm cool," I lied, hitting the blunt a few times before passing it back. "I'm just not tryna be up in here too long."

"Nah, you ain't cool my nigga, but I know what yo problem is."

"Really? And what's that?" I wanted to know. He looked at me like my ass was dumb.

"You need some pussy nigga! I know you ain't had none since you and shorty broke up, and it's fuckin with yo mental for real." He nodded like he was convinced of what he was saying, and I had to admit that he might have been on to something. The last time I had got my dick wet was the day of the party and, ever since then, shit had been going downhill. I wasn't the type that let pussy control my day to day, but I for damn sure wasn't used to not getting it when I wanted.

"You might be right."

"Might be? Nigga, I know I'm right! Yo ass need to just gone head and get back with yo girl, cause that's what you really want to do anyway." He cut me off and took a drink from his bottle of D'usse. I was sure my face showed my confusion at what the fuck Nivea had to do with this shit. I ain't need her to get no pussy! "Don't look at me like that man, if you wanted some new pussy, you would have gotten some by now! Yo ass want Nivea, and ain't shit wrong with that. When you find the one you wanna be with, don't let a bunch of bullshit get in the way."

I can't lie, a nigga was speechless. Troy wasn't the type of nigga that talked about feelings and all that shit. He was usually with a different bitch every night of the week, sometimes even twice a night. It was clear that fucking around with Niyah had him acting different, and that shit was a good look on him, but not when it came to me and Nivea though. I was still a little confused about that whole situation and I refused to believe that he had more clarity on it than me.

"I don't want Nivea nigga! Shorty made her decision and, if dude hadn't put his hands on her, she would still be over there with his snitch ass!" Just saying it out loud had me pissed off at her and him.

"Oh, so you just choosin not to fuck nothin?" He barely gave me a chance to say shit before he started again. "Hell naw! Yo ass not tryna mess with another bitch cause you waitin to get back with Nivea ass!" He was up in here sounding like a damn lawyer and shit and looking real proud of himself. I could tell that he was expecting for me to say something to further prove him right or, worse, try and argue the point so that he could continue to give his theories on the shit. I wasn't trying to do either. The ride was much better when his ass was off in his phone talking shit on his live.

"We've arrived." The driver came on and interrupted whatever it was that Troy was about to say. That was all he needed to hear to end the conversation and get back in turn up mode. I finished off my bottle while he straightened out his shirt and got ready to get out of the limo. The driver opened the door for us, and I stepped out first since I was the closest to the door. As soon as I hit the sidewalk, a chorus of screams emerged from the line of women that were outside.

"Savage!"

"Let me have yo baby Ju!"

"Take me home Trigga!"

"Who said that I'm tryna see somthin?" this nigga asked, getting out behind me and looking through the crowd, like he was really gone take one of their asses home with him.

"Nigga, bring yo ass on!" I laughed while leading the way with a bouncer beside me. I hadn't wanted the extra security, but Mone had insisted since we were getting bigger and I just rolled with it since I wasn't in the mood to go back and forth with his ass.

"Yo ass a hater," he huffed but gave up his search and continued into the club behind me, immediately forgetting about the girl outside. There was wall to wall bitches inside and they were lined up near the entrance grabbing at us. "Oh shit!"

I tried not to get too rough with any of these hoes, but I ain't like them putting their hands on me. The weak ass security that they had hired could barely handle them and another two or three big ass niggas had to come up to help us through the rest of the way to VIP.

Once we were finally seated in the club's little ass VIP section, which was on a balcony overlooking the floor, the owner came over and introduced himself. Right away, I could tell he was a grease ball ass nigga. He was dressed in a dark blue suit with a bright pink ass shirt underneath that was unbuttoned damn near half way down and some white boots. No lie, the nigga had on white boots. I held in a laugh as he stuck out his hand to me.

"Hey Savage, I'm Antonio! I'm glad you fellas decided to come out tonight!" he said, finally pulling his hand back once he realized that I wasn't about to touch his ass. "Whatever you guys want is on the house tonight! And I brought treats!" he let us know, moving aside so that a couple of big booty hoes could come into view.

"Bet, send one of yo bottle girls up here with some D'usse." I kept it short and then made my way over to one of the three white couches he had set up, up there. Troy, on the other hand, grabbed two of the bitches by hand and led them over to the couch opposite me. The other two girls stood around looking stupid, until they finally came over and took a seat on each side of me.

"Heyyy Ju," the ugliest of the two cooed, putting a hand on my shoulder.

"Nah, I'm straight," I let her know, shrugging away from her.

"But, you don't even know what I was bouta say."

"Yeah, I do, and like I said, I'm straight," I said coolly. I was trying not to hurt the ugly bitch feelings but, if she kept pushing me, I would tell her that her face and her breath had me about to throw up. Sucking her teeth, she stood up and went over to the couch that Troy and her other thot friends were on. I was expecting that the bitch she came over with was going to try and shoot her shot next but, without prompting, she took her ass over to where Troy was too.

The bottle girl came right after that with a tray that had three fifths of D'usse on it. I waited until she carefully sat them down before handing her a hundred dollar tip and grabbing up one for myself. After motioning for her to keep them coming, I cracked my bottle open and took a big sip. This club had me on edge. I wasn't sure if it was my mood prior to getting there or me just tweaking, but the shit didn't feel right. Troy didn't seem to notice shit since he was over there surrounded by hoes. I couldn't do shit but shake my head at that fool. He was just in the car trying to school me about some shit with my girl and he was up in here like he ain't have one.

"Man, yo ass up here killin the vibe Savage! All these bitches and drinks and yo ass still over there lookin depressed, my nigga! Fuck is wrong with you!" he questioned before the girl in his lap put his face between her titties.

"Fuck yo vibe nigga! If Niyah was here, it wouldn't be no fuckin vibe while you out here flexxin like you single!" He waved me off with a laugh like I was joking, but the mention of Niyah's name had him sliding shorty off his lap on the sly. I just grinned at his ass and went over to the balcony.

"Give it up for my nigga's Ju Savage and Trigga Troy slidin through tonight!" the DJ said over the screams from the crowd, and cut to our latest single "Glock Talk" before shining a bright ass light into our section. I flashed a gracious smile like the image guy that Mone had hired told me to and returned to my regular mug as soon as the light was out of my face.

After blinking like twenty times, my eyes finally adjusted

to the darkness of the club again and I looked out over the crowd below. That same bad feeling came over me as I watched people dancing and having fun. I turned to let Troy know and was shocked to see that he was standing next to me, leaned over the balcony, and throwing money down to the people directly under us.

"Aye man." I tapped his arm lightly to gain his attention.

"Wassup?" He barely looked my way as he continued to rain twenty dollar bills into the air. The bitches that had been all over him just a second before were now gone, and I wondered if his guilty conscious had him to send them away.

"I gotta bad feelin' man, you got yo joint on you?"

This time, he gave me his full attention "Hell yeah! I always got my baby mama with me." He lifted his shirt and showed me the chrome handle. "But what you mean? You see some shit I don't see?"

"Nah, I don't *see* shit, but I feel like somethin gone kick off, so just keep yo eyes and ears open," I told him and he nodded his understanding. Not even a second later, chaos erupted on the dance floor.

"Oh shit! It's goin down! Y'all hoes can't never come out and act right!" the DJ came over the speaker, cutting the music as a big ass crowd rushed over to the scene. From what I could see, it was two hoes out there fighting on the floor. I couldn't make out what they looked like because the crowd around them was so thick, but I saw that the one in the shiny ass nude dress was giving the other bitch the business.

It took them a minute before security could muscle their way through but, when they finally pulled them apart, I got a clear view of the one in the nude dress face and I couldn't fucking believe it.

"Nivea!"

CHAPTER 17

*N*ivea

"That's what the fuck I'm talkin bout best friend! Get yo fuckin hands off her!" Niyah was trying to fight the security as they pulled me and Pumpkin apart. I was pissed that I had even let this bitch get me to the point that I was in the fucking club fighting, when I was trying to be discreet and leave at the mention of Judah being there. I could almost bet that his yellow ass was up in VIP right then watching me make a damn fool out of myself.

"Bitch, I want my round! You snuck me!" Pumpkin hollered from the other side of the circle we were in. I had definitely fucked her ass up. She had blood leaking from her nose and into her mouth, making her wounds look worse than they actually were, but I knew her ass was gone have a black eye in the morning.

"You got yo round hoe and yo ass lost! Fuck you mean, my bitch ain't gotta sneak nobody and you better get yo fat ass back before I give you this work too hoe!" Niyah fussed at Cre, waving her shoes around that she had taken off at the start of the argument. Of course since it would have been a fair fight, Cre didn't want to act tough like she would have if it was just me there. Despite the embarrassment, I couldn't help but feel a little proud of myself for standing up to Pumpkin's ugly ass. But, just as the pride swelled in my chest, I caught sight of Judah storming his way through the slew of people with a mug that let me know he wasn't pleased.

"Aye yo, put her the fuck down!" he barked at the security guard that was holding onto me and, like Judah signed his checks, he did exactly as he was told and placed me gently on my feet.

"Judah, I-,"

"I ain't tryna hear that shit! What you doin in here showin yo ass for these bitches!" He grabbed ahold of my arm and pulled me to him, yelling into my face. "This the type of shit you was on with yo baby daddy! Huh!"

"Why the fuck do you even care!" I shouted back and snatched away from his hold. I wasn't even going to argue with him until he came at me all reckless and shit. The nerve of him to not be talking to me but have a problem with anything that I was doing. His ass was truly playing fucking games, and I wasn't about to sit and let him talk to me any kind of way.

"Nivea, stop playin with me, ayite! Let's fuckin go! Now!" Without waiting for me to reply, he began to pull me through the throng of people and towards the exit. I could see Niyah off to the side arguing with Troy, before he snatched her off of her feet and threw her over his shoulder. She didn't seem too happy about him yanking her ass out the club either, but she ain't have nobody but herself to blame since she insti-gated the fight and brought attention to us. I really could have slapped her extra loud ass.

Judah damn near bulldozed his way through the club until we reached the sidewalk right out front and, again, I snatched away from him, hoping that his grip on my arm would loosen up a bit, but he had a death grip on me.

"Judah, let me go before I scream out here!" I threatened and I meant it too; I'd act like his ass was killing me and, when the police came, I'd fall the fuck out. If his ass wanted to play games, I could too.

"Who the fuck gone run up on me, Nivea? Ain't a soul in these streets that got enough heart to try me to my face! Be the reason a nigga get smoked out here!" he said through clenched teeth with his nose damn near touching mine, he was so close. The look in his eyes told me not to test him, and I instinctively shrunk away. Regardless of the doubt I had in his innocence, I never thought that he would hurt me for real, now I wasn't so sure though.

He must have realized that he had my ass shook because his face softened a little, but he still didn't release my arm. "Go get the car nigga!" I hadn't noticed that their driver was standing beside us until he said that.

"Sorry, right away Sir," the man said timidly and disappeared in the direction I assumed the car was in.

"Let me the fuck go Troy!" Niyah hollered, drawing my attention away from Judah's steely gaze.

"Girl, you better calm the fuck down before I slam yo tough ass out here!" Troy had sat her down on her feet by now and was holding her while she twisted around in his arms and swung at him. The whole scene was a mess and the few remaining people that hadn't made it into the club, yet were out there with their phones out and aimed in our direction.

"Aye Savage!"

In the split second that he turned to see who had called him, gunfire erupted and he knocked me to the ground, covering my body with his. Judah started firing back, as dozens of screaming people ran for cover. It felt like forever before the shooting finally ceased, but it was really only about five minutes. By the time it was over, the street was filled with the sound of police sirens.

"Nivea? Nivea, you okay shorty?" Judah questioned, lifting himself off of me and checking over my body to make sure I wasn't hit. I nodded, unable to talk; even I was shaken up and sore from the impact of him pushing me out of the way. Relief covered his face briefly before he leaned in to peck my lips and then began looking around at all of the chaos going on.

"Aye Troy! Troy!" he shouted, since we couldn't see him through the crowd of people milling around us.

"I'm good Ju, stop fuckin yellin my government around this muthafucka!" we heard from across the way. Leave it to his ass to be talking shit right after a near death experience. Sometimes, I didn't know how him and Judah were such good friends. I watched Judah release a visible sigh of relief before helping me to my feet. Then, almost as if he was summoned, the driver pulled up at that moment and went to step out, but Judah shook his head no at him as Troy and Niyah came into view.

"Niyah!"

"Nivea!"

I broke away from Judah and ran over to where she was, wrapping my arms around her tightly.

"Biiitch! I'm sooooo glad you're okay!" she said tearfully.

"Me toooo!" I cried, trying to hold back my own tears. I'd lived in Chicago my whole life and had never been so close to people shooting. My body was shaking almost uncontrollably as we stood there hugging each other, and I could feel Niyah's heart pounding away too.

"Aye, look man, y'all can hug on each other in the limo; we gotta go before the reporters and the police show up," Troy quipped, looking around like he was watching out for them as he spoke. Niyah pulled away first while smacking her lips at him, but she still got into the open door he was holding for us, and I was right behind her.

As soon as Judah got inside, he came and sat right next to me, pulling me into his chest and kissing my forehead. We may have been arguing just a moment before but, the second the possibility arose where we might actually lose each other, that shit was over with. I snuggled closer to him, inhaling the scent of his 'Creed' cologne and relishing in the fact that I was in his arms after everything we'd been through. Being so close to him now had me forgetting about all of the things that had been said and done in the last couple of weeks, and I could barely remember why I was even worried about his innocence in the first place.

"Aye Troy? Tell me you peeped that shit, right?" Judah's deep voice vibrated through his chest, further comforting me, but I couldn't help perking up at the tone of his voice. He may have been stroking my back lovingly, but anger was radiating off of him damn near to the point that he was shaking.

"Hell yeah, that shit need to be handled asap," Troy spoke ominously and it was clear to me that they were speaking in code, well trying to anyway. I may not have known who they were talking about, but I knew that they were referring to the shooter. My eyes popped open and me and Niyah met each other's gaze across the limo. She too had found comfort in her man, despite her earlier resentment but, at the hint of something brewing, she was alerted just like me, except she was nosy enough to ask.

"What is you talkin about Troy? Who need to be handled? Yo ass barely recovered from the last time and you already tryna go get into some more shit!" she fussed, sitting up so that she was facing him.

"You know what the fuck I'm talkin bout Niyah, don't act

like you don't know what type of nigga I am! And in case you ain't noticed, niggas don't give a fuck! They could've hit you, and I don't play them type of games! I'm a man about mine, you always come before me and, if niggas out here willing to shoot at us knowing that you right there, then they willin to die wherever I catch em!"

"Well, do I at least get to know who it was since y'all both know? Me and Nivea's lives were just in danger too!" Troy looked Judah's way and Judah shook his head and blew out a deep breath.

"That's how you feel? Like you wanna know?" he asked, lifting my chin up towards him. Nodding, I shifted in the seat and sat up a little. I could see the conflict brewing in his eyes and wondered why me knowing who had shot at him would be such an issue, but I ain't have to wonder for long.

"It was Quad," he finally said after a minute of studying my face. I couldn't lie, Quad was the last name that I expected to come out of his damn mouth and a series of emotions ran through me right then. It was hard for me to believe that Quad hated Judah so much that he'd risk my life just to get at him. But, if I was being honest with myself, Quad had been shown me a whole mother side of him, even before he'd choked me that day.

"Oooh! That bitch ass nigga! He look like he'd do some hoe ass shit like that!" Niyah shrieked at the mention of his name. "You should've shot him in his ass!"

I wanted to laugh, but there wasn't shit funny about my children's father trying to kill me on more than one occasion. I kept trying to come up with reasons why it couldn't have been him but, the longer I thought about it, the more obvious it was that he definitely would and both Judah and Troy must have seen him too.

"You straight?" Judah asked softly, knowing the turmoil I

was going through after hearing something like that. I shrugged, even though I wanted to cry.

"As straight as I can be, considering." I didn't want to dwell too long on the fact that I was beyond hurt about Quad's recent actions. It was bad enough I'd let him separate us like Judah was such a danger to society, when he was the one putting our family at risk every time I turned around.

"You ain't gotta pretend like it don't bother you that yo baby daddy pulled some bitch shit like this. I ain't so cold hearted that I can't understand how something like this might fuck up yo mental, and I won't say I told you so either; y'all got kids and shit. Plus, he been good as fuck at hiding his true nature from yo green ass. At this point though, ion even trust that nigga around the kids... do he know where yo mama live?" he asked as an afterthought.

"Oh, my God, yes! I gotta go get the kids and my mama!"

"I'll kill that fuckin nigga!" Judah spat icily before he dropped the partition so that he could give the driver my Mom's address. I silently prayed that he didn't take his ass anywhere near my babies in the deranged state he was in.

It took us less than twenty minutes to arrive at my Mama's house where all of the lights were off. Frantically, I ran inside with Judah, Niyah and Troy right behind me with their guns drawn ready for anything.

I went to my old bedroom to find all of the kids in the bed snoring and breathed a sigh of relief. It was clear that Quad hadn't been there, but I wasn't about to take any chances, not tonight anyway. I shook both of the girls awake so they could slip on something to wear outside, then quickly dressed QJ's little sleeping body and he didn't even stir.

"Ma, where we goin?" Quiana asked, still half asleep.

"Obviously runnin from yo daddy again dummy," Ky sneered.

"Now ain't the time Ky! Y'all done getting dressed; y'all can go down to the car with Judah." At the sound of his name, both girls perked up and literally ran to where he was standing just outside the bedroom, shrieking happily. I could hear them asking him questions like it wasn't the middle of the night.

When I came out with QJ, he took him from my arms. "I'm gone take them to the limo, you gone grab yo mama." And before I could even say anything, he was jogging down the stairs with the girls following closely behind at the mention of a limo.

"Nivea? What the fuck you makin all that noise for at this time of night?" I turned and my mama was already standing in the hallway behind me, tying up her robe with an irritated expression covering her face. It shouldn't have surprised me that they had woken her up; my mama was an extremely light sleeper and heard everything.

"I'm sorry ma, but we need to get out of here, now," I emphasized.

"Well, just wait till in the morning, it don't make sense to take them outta here this late at night."

"Naw, you don't understand ma; we need to leave because it's not safe, at least for the night," I added, once I saw her about to argue but that didn't stop her.

"What the fuck you mean leave for the night? What the hell y'all done did? It bet not be shit illegal and you brought yo ass here!" I blew out an exasperated breath as she continued to fuss. "Who you with, that damn Quad?"

"Oh, my God, ma, Quad just shot at us at the club and I know he saw me out there, but that didn't stop him! So yes, we need to leave before he bring his crazy ass over here!" I finally cut her off and said. That instantly silenced her and her eyes bucked in surprise.

"Oh, hell naw! That nigga done really lost his mind!"

"Exactly, so can you just come on. We're going to Judah's house, just for the night hopefully."

She grunted her response and thankfully went to go get dressed, talking shit the whole way. I waited until she came back out dressed in some pink sweats and gym shoes. My nerves were shot, but I was starting to calm down a little.

"Wait, where's Nadia?" I asked before we made it out the door.

"Oh, she's at her new boyfriend's house for the night chile." She waved her hand flippantly. Judah stood on the porch leaned up against the rail like he was just waiting for some shit to kick off.

"How you doin Ms. Hynes?" he greeted, unsmiling as he waited for us to go down the stairs first.

"I've been better." I rolled my eyes at her wishy washy ass. Just the other day she was singing the nigga praises and, now, in his presence, she was being short with him. It could have been because of the fact that she was woken up at three in the damn morning, but I doubted it. Judah either didn't seem to notice or he wasn't worried about it right then because he merely nodded and continued to lead us to the limo. The tension inside was now gone since Kymia and Quiana were wide awake and oohing and ahhhing over everything, but we were all still preoccupied with the night's events as we pulled off.

CHAPTER 18

*N*iyah

Who would have thought that the night would've turned out so fucking crazy? I should have known though because whenever Savage and Nivea were in the same space, some wild shit always happened. I swear, they needed their own "Love and Hip Hop show". That's really why I was going so hard to get them back together. Nivea ain't know it, but I knew that the fellas were going to be at club Ki$$, and I'd been planning on him seeing her looking all good and shit with another nigga in her face. What I hadn't planned on was seeing Pumpkin and her sister ill built asses. The minute they announced that Savage was in the building, Nivea was ready to get her sprint on and do the hundred meter dash up out that bitch. I'd tried to convince her that he wouldn't even know she was there since he was in VIP, even though I had full intentions on drawing his attention her way. She still really wasn't trying to hear that shit though and was in the middle of explaining that to me when Pumpkin walked up talking shit. As Nivea's best friend, I knew how she felt about acting a fool in public, but I wasn't the one! Wasn't no bitch large, small, fat or skinny about to talk shit to me and get away with it and the same went for my friend. So, as soon as that bitch started talking reckless about their punk ass baby daddy getting his ass beat by Savage, I had no choice but to show my ass. For one, I knew Nivea could beat that bitch ass on her worse day and, for two, it would definitely let Judah know we was in the building so, in my eyes, it was a win, win.

Everything played out exactly how I thought it would too! Nivea fucked that hoe up and Savage came down there and got his woman. I knew that I would have to deal with Troy's extra ass, but it was worth it to make my girl get her "love all over me" glow back. What I wasn't expecting though was for Quad's stupid ass to come and try to kill some-damn-body! I was way too young to die and especially at the hands of his backwards ass. If there was any way that I could be present when they finally laid that nigga to rest, I'd probably pull the trigger before Savage or Troy could.

"Aye, we here," Troy said, gently shaking me out of my sleep. I still wanted to pretend like I had an attitude with him, but being so close to death had me ready to stop the games. I just hoped that it had the same effect on him. Everyone else was already getting out by the time, I realized that we weren't at Troy's apartment.

"Judah, I thought we were going to your place? I ain't tryna have these kids mess up this house," Nivea questioned, stopping him as he attempted to carry QJ inside. A funny expression covered his face before he looked back at all of us.

"The kids straight, this my spot."

I had to give it to my girl, she held her composure good as fuck, cause I know her jaw wanted to touch the ground. I looked at Troy, confused myself, and he just shrugged like it wasn't a big deal. I guess when you sign with a major label, buying mini mansions and Audi's ain't shit to you. He grabbed ahold of my hand and led me inside where the girls were running around like it wasn't early as fuck in the morning.

I looked around admiring how neat it was in there, despite the fact that it looked like a trap nigga house. All that covered the massive living room was a huge black, leather sectional, matching ottomans and a big ass flat screen hung on the wall. It was so damn empty in there that the girls voices echoed off the walls of the foyer.

"Quiana! Kymia! Please sit down somewhere!" Nivea snapped.

"Come on, I'ma show y'all where y'all sleeping," Savage said, but pounding at the door stopped everybody from going up the stairs behind him, even the girls stopped. He handed Quad Jr. to Nivea and nodded for her to go towards the back.

"Come on girls." They quickly took off behind their mother with Ms. Hynes, while I stood there waiting to see who it was. I wasn't the toughest but, like I'd said earlier, I wanted to be present if it was Quad's hoe ass. Troy bucked his eyes at me and I bucked mine right back, prompting him to release a heavy sigh before pulling his gun. I couldn't help smirking cause he knew not to say shit to me.

"Oh, hell naw!" My cousin being on the other side of the door was the last thing I expected. I had been seeing a lot of her lately because she'd been using my mama as her own personal baby sitter and chef, so she was always there.

"Ugh, what's she even doin here?" She frowned at the sight of me. "Can we please talk in private Savage?"

"Bitch, you got yo nerve! Wait- where the fuck the girls at?" I finally realized that she didn't have them with her. She looked back nervously and then pleaded with Savage to come outside, so they could talk.

"Hell naw, I ain't goin nowhere wit yo crazy ass! How the

fuck you even know where I live anyway!" he told her. "Didn't I tell you to stay the fuck away from me anyway!" She looked stunned by his tone, but she had to expect that considering that she had drugged him and tried to ruin his relationship the last time he saw her.

"Obviously, I followed y'all from the club and get used to seeing me around because this baby needs a father!"

"Bitch, you know damn well I ain't never been up in you raw; you better go find the real nigga responsible and get the fuck on!"

"That's why you brought yo dumb ass back around? I knew you was on some ole sneaky ass shit the minute you showed up at my mama house!" Troy and Savage both turned to me, confused as hell.

"How you know her?" Troy questioned, pointing his gun between me and her.

"This my nutty ass cousin," I told him, sucking my teeth in irritation.

"I'm crazy for lovin' my man? Hmph, no wonder yo ass can't keep one!" Kisha yelled from her spot at the door, drawing my attention back to her.

"Bitch, I will body yo goofy ass! You nutty cause you go around druggin niggas and beatin on yo kids! Wait till I talk to Kenyon! I know damn well he ain't give you them kids!" I still hadn't talked to him yet, and I was starting to think this crazy ass girl had done something to him. I only threw out his name to see what type of reaction she'd have, but there was none. Her face remained unbothered by what I'd said.

"Kids? What fuckin kids!" Savage's face contorted angrily as he looked back and forth between the two of us.

"You wanna tell him or should I?" I was more than prepared to give him the tea on her because it was obvious he didn't know shit about her besides that she sings.

"I have two daughters. They lived with their daddy up

until a few weeks ago when he signed over his rights to me. I ain't think you wanted kids cause you always sayin you too young for this or that, so I never told you about them. But now that we're having a baby, I feel like you should meet them. You've gotten practice playin house with that hoe, now we can be a real family." She nudged her chin toward the back with a grin, and we all turned to see Nivea looking just as confused as we did.

"Yo, this bitch really crazy man!" Troy shook his head and mumbled under his breath. I didn't know how they hadn't figured that shit out yet. Even without them knowing about her abusing kids, crazy people couldn't keep it in check too long before they finally snapped.

"Girrrrl, tonight really ain't the night to be fuckin with me. I already owe you one, don't test me," Nivea said calmly, coming into the foyer with us. I didn't know what it was but Nivea had that fed up tone going on and it was an instant warning for Kisha because she went back to talking to Savage and kept Nivea out of it.

"You gotta at least give me and my kids a chance Savage! I-"

"Kisha, man listen, I ain't tryna fuck with you like that. I been told yo ass that and, months later, you still trying. I'm tryin not to put my fuckin hands on you, get yo ass away from here." Savage pinched the bridge of his nose as he spoke, clearly finding it hard to deal with the situation.

"Are you kidding me? After everything I did for you, you think you can just make me go away! Do you have any fuckin idea what I had to do to get them damn kids! They been drivin me crazy since I took them! Always hungry, can't stay clean, always whinin for their damn daddy! I'm ready to smother them lil muthafuckas in their sleep because of you and you still don't want me!" She started wailing and pulling at her hair like the crazy bitch she was.

"You know what! Since yo ass the reason I even took these lil bastards, you can have them!" She turned on her heels before anyone could object and, the next thing we knew, she was dragging them up the steps and damn near slung them through the doorway.

"Aw bitch, you got me fucked up!" I ran past Troy and Savage and punched her right in her mouth, knocking her backwards off of the porch. She landed on her back and hurried to scramble to her feet, but I was already coming down the stairs behind her.

"Niyah, don't! She said she pregnant!" I could hear everything that Nivea was saying, but the minute that hoe said all that shit and threw them kids like that she was asking for it in my mind anyway, but just because of the baby, I only hit her in the face. By the time I was finally pulled off of her, she was unrecognizable. Everybody was screaming out shit behind me as I was hoisted away and into the house, while Nivea sat on the phone with the police. She was better than me though cause I would have let her ass bleed out right there on the ground; her ass was probably lying about being pregnant anyway. I didn't know that it was Troy who'd grabbed me until he hemmed me up in the corner with a shit-eating grin on his face.

"Calm yo ass down baby Mayweather."

"Boy, I am calm! Where her kids at? I wanna see them before the police get here cause if they got one scratch on em, I'ma go beat her ass some more!" He let me go and stepped aside so that I could see my two cousins sitting on the couch now wide awake and in tears. I was ready to go outside and bring Kisha's ass back just to fuck her up again. It was clear that these kids had been getting their asses beat, and I honestly didn't know how my mama hadn't seen the marks that covered their arms and faces. My heart broke in half seeing them that way and knowing that the whole time they were with that bitch, I knew something wasn't right but didn't say anything. I didn't realize I was crying with them until Troy came over and touched my shoulder as I kneeled in front of them, holding onto them tightly.

"Don't cry Niyah man, you gone make me go murk that bitch just for havin tears in yo eyes." That was the best pep talk I would get out of his tough ass and I knew it, so I just nodded as tears still streamed down my face. Guilt was eating me alive. I barely managed to get the girls calmed down by the time I heard the police at the door. Troy had already gone to make sure I wasn't arrested but, instead of staying there, I went to the door and I was gonna proudly take that charge with a smile in my mugshot.

The front door was still wide open and Troy sat on the bottom step while Nivea and Savage stood talking to the officers by the squad car. I could hear him going off about how she popped up at his house, and they better get her crazy ass before he shoot her. Nivea was trying to calm him down, but it was obvious that he had, had all the drama he could take for the night. The officers finally realized that they weren't going to get a real statement out of them and closed up their little tablets and went to walk off when the driver stopped.

"Aw yeah... umm what happened to her before we got here?" His ass was trying to be funny because that should have been one of the first questions he asked.

"Shiiit, she fell down the stairs."

"She fell or did somebody push her?" the officer pressed with a smug grin.

"If I had pushed that bitch down the stairs, she'd be leavin on a stretcher, not in your squad car... good night pig," Savage told him and started back towards the house, leaving dude ass stuck. I couldn't help but laugh once we'd closed the door and Troy looked at me like I was crazy.

"Bring yo crazy ass on man." He wrapped an arm around my neck and pulled me close to him so that Savage could show us to where we were sleeping. I didn't know what Nivea had told them to stop them from calling DCFS tonight to come and pick up the kids, but I knew that at some point I would have to figure out what to do with them. My mama was too old for kids and, me, I wasn't ready to raise anyone besides myself. I'd have to either find Kenyon or they would go to a foster home.

CHAPTER 19

*T*roy

"Aye man, there he go," I alerted Savage as we sat outside of the Goon Squads manager's office. This whole time we had been trying to keep a lot of people out of the mix because it would be less witnesses and less bodies that we'd have to deal with, especially considering the deal we had. It wasn't that we were moving different or no shit like that but we did have to move smarter, and pulling up at niggas' houses or businesses wasn't smart in the position we were in. But, desperate times were calling for desperate measures and we were fucking beyond desperate. Keys dry snitching ass hadn't made any appearances and had left his group mates to fend for themselves, trying to explain his absence without giving away the fact that he was a state's witness. We'd already went to them niggas and they'd spilled their guts about that shit and also put a bug in our ear that the nigga had slipped his security and had really disappeared. Supposedly, their manager Rome had given them that information and so it made me feel like his ass knew more. I mean, why would the fucking police contact him to let him know that Keys had gotten away? He knew about him getting out of protective custody because Keys had let him know, *personally.*

Rome stepped out of his office building looking like he was dodging a nigga he owed money to. We waited until he had almost made it to our car before we got out. As soon as he saw us, he stopped walking and looked around for a way to escape, but there was none.

"Look guys, I don't know where Keys is," he said, immediately throwing up his hands in defense.

"See, I knew yo ass was gone say somethin like that. Didn't I call it Troy?" Savage cocked his head and asked.

"You sholl fuckin did," I agreed with a nod as I pulled a twenty from my pocket. We'd bet on what this nigga would do once we got there and I just knew his ass was gone run, but Savage bet that he would try and say he ain't know dude's whereabouts. We ain't even have a gun pointed at him and he stood there with his hands in the air while I handed off Savage's winnings to him. He took it with a grin and shoved it in his pocket.

"Come holla at us Rome," he said coolly, the light mood gone.

"I uhhh, I was on my way to a meeting actually, I-"

"Nigga, that wasn't no fuckin request! Get yo bitch ass over here!" I snapped with my face balled up. His ass was out here trying to make a deal, knowing damn well that shit wasn't gone fly. He jumped at my tone and Savage's ass chuckled.

"Nigga, you impatient as fuck." He shook his head at me, and I just shrugged. I'd be impatient if that meant we got this shit over with. All I was trying to do was make music and fuck on Niyah's little sexy ass, but these niggas had me out here doing shit that a nigga like me supposed to had left behind. I would be a thug until I died, but that ain't mean I

136

always wanted to deal with bullshit beef. To think that this shit all started because we put a nigga out the studio. That was muthafuckas problem now, they didn't respect the next man's hustle.

Rome walked his scary ass over shaking like a leaf and looking as if he was going to try some shit, so I pulled my gun out and pointed it at him discreetly. That time of night it wasn't too busy over here, but I wasn't going to take any chances.

"Don't do nothin stupid Rome," I warned. The sight of the gun caused him to pause for a second, but he was already within arm's reach, so I yanked him over to me by the collar of his suit jacket. I led him to the car and shoved him into the backseat, sliding in behind him as Savage got in the driver's seat.

"I'm really upset that I had to go to these measures to find Keys, Rome," Savage said once he started driving.

"Look, I'm tellin you I don't know where his lil ass at! You think I'd be cool with him missin shows and appearances cause he runnin from y'all niggas? I don't get paid if they don't deliver! Ouch man, shit!" He let out after I slapped his ass upside the head.

"Nigga, shut up! I don't give a fuck about nothin but where Keys is at, and I know damn well CPD ain't call you up to say that nigga wasn't under their protection no more. So, either you gone tell us where he at or we gone take a trip to yo crib. Ain't this yo house?" I showed him a picture I had in my phone of the house he'd just moved his family into. "Don't yo bitch still work from home? She should be there right now, right?"

"Okay! Okay! My family don't got shit to do with this!"

"That's where you got this shit wrong at my nigga! Yo family became involved as soon as you decided to hide that nigga from me!" Savage spat, looking at him in the rear view.

This nigga must have really been scared as hell. He was sweating bullets and breathing hard as fuck.

"Aye man, spit that shit out for yo ass hyperventilate back here!" I ain't know shit about the healthcare field, but I know his ass wasn't supposed to be breathing like that.

"Ok! I... I... ummm, I put Keys in a hotel out in Aurora!" Savage and I looked at each other through the mirror, both of us suspicious of what he'd said.

"That shit sounded like a fuckin lie my nigga, and I'ma tell you know I hate being lied to, especially when I been askin for the truth so nicely."

"I swear! That's the truth!"

"Ayite then but, just in case, you get to ride with us and, if you lyin my nigga, that's gone be yo ass," I warned. "Tell him which hotel it is, so we can get on the road." I motioned toward Savage. Rome's eyes got big as hell as he looked between the two of us.

"I- I can't go right now! I told y'all I have a meetin, I can't-!" he stuttered.

"You can't or you won't cause you know it's a difference?" I questioned nonchalantly, opening up a text on my phone from Niyah. It was a picture of her at my crib sitting on my bed in a sheer black teddy, with the message: *hurry home daddy*. Her ass damn sure knew how to distract me.

I hit her right back and said, *it's gone be a minute, but if you fall asleep I'll wake you up.*

Without even seeing her face, I knew she was disappointed and she proved me right by sending a crying emoji.

I'll make it up to you. I promise.

"I'm, I'm not sayin I won't. I just can't do it today," he stressed like that shit meant anything to me.

"Ohhh, this nigga think we give a fuck about his schedule." Savage laughed from the front seat and I cackled right along with him.

"You think we care about anything on yo agenda? My bitch waiting for me right now and I'm stuck in here with yo sweaty ass! The only thing that need to be comin out yo mouth right now is the location to this fuckin hotel, other than that I ain't tryna hear shit!" We could have found the hotel on our own, but we would still need to figure out that nigga's room number and it wasn't no telling what the fuck his alliance was. Besides, like I'd said, I wanted Rome's ass close cause if he was sending us off, I was gonna murk his ass.

By the time we'd taken the short drive out to Aurora, he had let us know that Keys was in the Aurora hotel under the alias of Antwon Fischer. You know we clowned the fuck out of him for that goofy ass shit as we made our way there.

"Ahhh, hell naw! Why you got that nigga in this raggedy ass hotel?" I questioned once the GPS had us pull into the parking lot. It was obvious from the outside alone that the inside wasn't shit and I felt bad for Keys' ass. We hadn't even been expecting the nigga to leave town, so he would have been safe in a four-star hotel.

"Shit, I take one nighters to better rooms than this shit! What y'all niggas pay by the hour in this bitch!"

"We thought it would be safer to go to a cheaper hotel," he said lowly, probably embarrassed and he should have been. This shit looked like bed bugs and roaches was gone jump us as soon as we stepped inside.

"I feel like we gone need a hazmat suit just to walk in that bitch!" Savage added from the front seat. "Man, text that nigga and tell him to come out! I ain't goin in there!" Rome looked my way to see if he was serious or not.

"I'm with Savage, text that nigga." He pulled his phone out of his pocket and shakily went to the messages. I watched him closely to make sure he ain't say too much besides that he was there and wanted to come up to his room. It didn't surprise me that Keys' scary ass insisted for him to come up instead of him coming outside. Rome looked to me like he wasn't sure. "Shit, I guess we gotta go up then."

We walked right alongside Rome, as he entered the lobby of the dingy hotel and only gave him space once he got off the elevator on the second floor.

"You think this shit legit?" I asked Savage in a low tone as we walked a few paces behind Rome. "That nigga answered back quick as hell."

"Shit, I'm ready for whatever; remember, Keys wasn't the toughest out the pack anyway, his ass probably up in there terrified. I told his stupid ass not to do no stupid shit like talk and that was the first thing he did when word got out about dude and his mama." His face was grim and I knew he was worried about handling this shit. I had to admit that I felt responsible to a certain degree, considering that he had risked his freedom on account of me. If I needed to handle this shit on my own, I would but, after so much shit happening, I knew he wanted his piece. We stopped just outside of room 211 and waited while Rome knocked.

"Who?" Keys' muffled voice came through the thick door. I knew his bitch ass was inspecting every inch of the small peephole that he could, but all that was visible was Rome's fat head ass.

"Rome, nigga, open the door!" Rome had nerve to have some bass in his voice as he said it. I looked at Savage standing on the other side of him and smirked; this dude was hilarious. The second the door creaked open, Savage pushed Rome inside and and stepped into view.

"Oh shit! Savage!" Keys screamed out, raising his hands up.

"Oh shit, Savage! Nigga, you sound like a whole bitch out here." I chuckled, coming into the room last and letting the door close behind me. Savage, who still hadn't pulled his gun, stood there just staring at Keys with dark eyes.

"Rome man, what the fuck!" Keys looked to his manager like he had betrayed him.

"They held me at gunpoint and threatened my family! I ain't have no fuckin choice!" Rome hissed back, standing next to him.

"What the fuck did I tell you, Keys? Didn't I say that I would come get you nigga?" Savage had the nigga standing there shaking and I knew if he raised his voice even a little bit, Keys would probably piss his pants. "Put yo shoes on, we bouta take a trip," he said calmly, prompting Keys to shake his head.

"Look Savage, you don't have to do this."

"Oh, I'm sposed to be cool with spending the remainder of my life in prison? You got me fucked up! Put yo damn shoes on and let's go before I just do yo ass here." Keys slowly looked around for his shoes, overlooking at least three pairs that was right in his face.

"Nigga, you see them damn shoes right there, quit playin like my nigga a joke!" I barked, and he hurried to put his feet in a pair of slides that were next to the nightstand. It was no wonder he could even find shit in that messy ass room. It was food cartons and garbage all over, mixed with clothes. The whole room wreaked of stale feet and moldy food, and I couldn't wait to go back out into fresh air.

After that nigga got his shoes on, we shuffled him and Rome out the door and, instead of using the front lobby, we went around and left through one of the side doors. The whole time, Keys was begging for his life, but he should have already known that he wasn't getting a pass. Not when he should have kept shit to himself but didn't.

"Can I go now? I did what y'all asked me to," Rome whined as soon as he realized we weren't walking back to the car. I decided not to answer him because he should have known at this point that we weren't leaving anymore witnesses. The closer we got to the edge of the parking lot, the more nervous he got and he was crying once we got to the part with the least amount of light. On some super hero shit, he tried to spin around real fast and grab my gun out of my hand and, on impulse, I released two bullets into his chest. He dropped instantly and I cursed cause his dumb ass had just made it so that we would have to hurry up. He was still alive and on the ground moaning, while Keys began to cry more loudly. Even though I knew he was going to die, I still fired one last shot right into the center of his forehead because I wasn't taking any chances. While Keys' attention was on me, Savage shot his ass straight through this right cheek and then another once he hit the ground behind his manager.

"Come on before somebody see us!" I grabbed the sleeve of Savage's hoodie and yanked his ass away. We walked as fast as we could without drawing attention to ourselves before people started exiting the hotel, trying to be nosy. I didn't really know too much about Aurora, but we were on our way back before the sound of police sirens erupted the night. I'd told my shorty that I wasn't going to be too long, so I was hoping she hadn't took her ass to sleep, cause I was still gone keep my promise of waking her ass up.

CHAPTER 20

*S*avage
     Smoking that nigga Keys had been a burden off my shoulders and now I could breathe a little better knowing that there was only one more problem to eliminate. Though we had to go through a few avenues, it hadn't been too hard to find Keys, but that nigga Quad was slipping through the cracks and I knew it was because he'd stayed under the police's guard. I wasn't going to trip though, because he was obviously following us with the intentions of getting me before I got him, so I would be seeing him soon. And this time, I would be more than prepared. Since he still had yet to be found though, I'd made that the excuse I had to keep Nivea and the kids close, which meant that they were still staying at the house I'd bought for them. She still didn't know that I had originally gotten it in hopes of us all living there, but she was happy that there was room for everyone. Her mama had gone home the next day after all that shit had happened because in her words, she wasn't scared of bitch ass Quad. I'd tried to get her to stay, but she wasn't going for that shit. She wanted her privacy and she gave me the vibe

that she had a man on the low. Nivea argued me up and down that it ain't no man messing with her mama, but she would see soon.

"Aye, put some more bass in there," I told the producer. I was in the studio working on a mixtape. It had been a couple of days since we had gotten rid of Keys and the news had already been reporting on the incident. As far as I knew, they didn't have any suspects, but I knew that eventually the police would bring their asses around to question me in connection to the shit just because he was a witness on my case. That's another reason why I'd secured an alibi with the studio's time log.

I let the sound of the instruments in the background flow through my headphones with the added bass for a few seconds before I got ready to spit the sixteen bars I had written for the music, when the door to the studio was pushed open and in walked two dicks. I smirked at them, knowing that they would come eventually and took off the headphones.

"Hey, I said y'all can't come in here like that!" Scotty, the producer I was working with, shouted as he followed them into the booth.

"It's cool Scotty," I told him and he quieted down, but he still looked bothered by their presence. "What can I help y'all with?"

"Were you aware that a Keyshawn "Keys" McCullen was found murdered, along with his manager?" the shorter of the two asked gruffly, already in a hostile mood. I could tell he was going to be playing the tough cop role.

"Yeah, I saw that on the news this mornin, shit sad." I faked sympathy and shook my head like I really gave a fuck, causing the officer's eyes to narrow.

"Well, it's not really too bad for you now, is it Mr. Ju Savage?"

"Excuse me?"

"You were aware of the fact that Mr. McCullen was going to testify against you in your upcoming trial, right?" He stepped further into the room as if that would intimidate me, but I was extremely cool.

"No, as a matter of fact I wasn't. As far as I knew, the only witness was a nigga named Quad." I shrugged.

"You're a god damn lie! We're gonna find out that you had something to do with this! And when we do, you're going down for four murders you son of a bitch!" he sneered angrily, trying to get past his partner so that he could be closer to me. His partner held him back and then pushed him towards the door.

"Hey! Hey! Calm down damnit! If you can't handle this, then you need to go wait for me in the car!" he shouted, finally getting him over the threshold and outside of the booth. This nigga's face was red as hell, he was so mad; you would have thought that I'd killed his people or something. I swear these white police officers were crazy as hell. They needed to do mental health tests on their asses.

"I'm cool!" The first one snatched away and stormed out, looking at me with a mug. I made sure to show all thirty two teeth when I smiled at him as he left, pissing him off even more. Once he was finally gone completely, the second one turned to me with a tight lipped expression. He hated my little ass and I knew that it was killing him to have to be nice, but he was obviously the more seasoned of the two.

"Sorry about my partner, he's new to the force," he explained like I gave a shit, which I didn't but I nodded, trying to seem understanding anyway.

"Well, as I was tellin yo partner, I've never seen dude name on any of my paperwork. The only thing I know about him is that we did a song with his group a few months back, but I haven't seen any of them since." He grit his teeth at my response, probably knowing damn well I knew exactly who Keys ass was.

"And do you have an alibi for two nights ago?"

"Yeah, I was here in the studio." The lie came out so smooth, you would have thought I really was in there working instead of in Aurora killing two niggas.

"Is there someone that can verify that for you?" He raised his eyebrows and leaned forward on his toes.

"Yeah, it's a sign in log at the front desk and Scotty was here too." I nudged my chin at Scotty, who was still standing in the doorway with his arms folded as he watched the exchange.

"And what time did you leave?"

"I went to the crib at about one, and my girl and her kids were there so she can vouch for me." I was already starting to get tired of his line of questioning, especially when I steady knew what his ass was gone ask.

"Why just her and not the kids?" he asked quickly like he'd caught me up.

"Cause the kids were sleep at one in the mornin- you know what, fuck this! I been answering all yo questions even though I ain't have to, and yo ass steady bullshittin! I don't know dude like that, and I got two alibis. Get yo ass up outta here before I call my lawyer nigga!" He looked like his partner had a minute before, but I wasn't worried about it. There wasn't shit that would tie me and Troy to that murder, so he could be as mad as he wanted.

"You might think you've slipped away Savage, but we still have a witness, so killing Keys really didn't help you at all. We'll be in touch." Despite the smirk on his face, I could see the hate that lived in his eyes. I really didn't know why CPD had such a hard on for me. Outside of the case with Quad, they had no knowledge of my wrongdoings.

"Okay, you done wasted enough of our studio time," Scotty finally said irritably.

"Like I said, I'll be back!" The detective huffed and turned on his heels, leaving the room almost as angry as his partner had been.

"They pressed ain't they?" Scotty said the minute the door slammed behind the detective.

"Shiiit, they on me more than the hoes be." I shrugged.

"Well, you know I can vouch for you being here, so don't even worry about that shit."

"Respect." I nodded and grabbed my headphones off of the microphone I'd sat them on. "Now, let's finish this track so I can take my ass home."

The visit from the jakes had only set us back a few minutes, so we were able to finish the song not even two hours later, and I was on my way to the crib. I weaved in and out of traffic bopping my head to some Future when my phone rang, cutting my shit off at my favorite part. At the sight of Mone's name, I started not to answer, but I knew his persistent ass would just keep calling back. Since we'd gotten the deal, he'd been on our asses more than before.

"Wassup Mone?"

"Don't wassup me, lil nigga! Tell me you ain't have shit to do with that lil goon squad nigga and his manager dyin!" I looked down at the screen in my car that displayed his name like he could see me and frowned. He had to have been stupid as hell to think that I would cop to some shit like that over the phone, let alone in person.

"I ain't have shit to do with that shit," I told him flatly.

"You better hope you didn't! Got fuckin detectives poppin up at my office and shit askin me questions! Where the fuck is Troy?" He was mad as hell! I could literally hear the spit flying out of his mouth as he spoke.

"Aye, calm all that shit down when you talkin to me, man!

147

I ain't got detectives doin shit, them niggas decided to come fuck with me on their own. As far as Troy, I don't know that nigga's whereabouts all the time!"

"Ayite man... relax."

"Naw, you relax, nigga don't forget who sign yo checks!" I paused to let that sink in for his ass and he obviously got the message because the rest of the conversation happened much more smoothly.

"Ayite man just, just stay out of trouble and relay the message to Troy cause I know he ignorin me." His tone came down.

"Bet," I said simply and disconnected the call. It was like everybody wanted to fuck with me that day. Just because my mood had lightened due to us having gotten Keys out the way didn't mean that I wasn't still the same old Savage.

I pulled up to the crib not too long after that, ready to spend what was left of the day with my girl and the kids. Nivea and me getting back together had made them happy as hell, and they had already started putting their rooms together in the house. Shit had almost gone back to the way that they were except I couldn't rest until I killed their father, and that always made me feel a little guilty when I was in their presence. But, Quad dying was inevitable. He'd violated on more than one occasion and his ass had to go to ensure that he wouldn't cause any more problems around me and Nivea.

"Hey Savage!" Kymia chirped happily as soon as I stepped foot into the kitchen, where she sat eating some cereal at the island.

"Wassup Ky?" Of all of the kids, she had been the one that I'd had spent time with the least. And it wasn't because of her attitude either, because a little mini teen's hormonal issues didn't bother me. I took a seat down at the island with her and leaned on my elbows across the top.

"Nothin, just tryin to get away from Quiana annoying butt," she grumbled, shoveling a spoonful of cereal into her mouth. I couldn't help but chuckle because I knew that Quiana's little ass was really annoying when she wanted to be.

"Let the lil diva live," I joked, making her roll her eyes.

"Right, she need to let all of us live."

"Well, I'm tellin you now my lil sister be on the same stuff, but she gone be there for life, so you might as well get used to her gettin on yo nerves. Try being a lil nicer to her tho, that might help." It took everything in me not to include curse words with that little speech and I was kind of proud that I'd managed without slipping up. I didn't know barely anything about kids. The little I did know, I'd picked up from my O.G. and Nivea recently, but it seemed like I was getting the hang of that shit.

"I guess I can try," she said reluctantly.

"Respect." I flashed her a grin and reached out for her to give me a dap, as I looked at a message from Troy.

"Hey ummm… Savage." Her voice had turned from the light cheery tone she'd had a second before, and now it was a little shaky. Real shit, I was almost scared to look up and see that her facial expression matched her voice.

"Call me Judah, but what's up?" I tried to sound nonchalant like I was barely listening, in hopes that maybe she wouldn't say whatever it was that was making her so uncomfortable.

"When you catch Quad, make sure he don't come back."

CHAPTER 21

*N*ivea

So, I'd officially given my apartment up and put all my stuff into storage until I had more time to sell it or whatever. Judah had given the girls a five thousand dollar budget each for them to decorate their rooms and they both were more than ready to spend his money. That day alone I'd already spent about half on their furniture shopping online and planned to finish the rest the next day. I never thought that shopping online would be so damn tiring, but it had me laid up in the bed with QJ with a crook in my neck watching old reruns of the Real Housewives of Atlanta. QJ wasn't really trying to settle down though and, when Judah stepped into the room, he jumped off the bed and ran over to him excitedly.

"Ju! Ju!" A smile instantly replaced the grim expression that had been on his face and I was glad that my kids could lighten his mood.

"What's up lil man?" he said, tickling him and then setting him back down on the. "Yo sister got some snacks for y'all downstairs, gone get some while I talk to yo mama." At the sound of snacks, QJ ran out of the room with a loud shout of happiness.

"What's wrong bae?" I asked, sitting up on my knees in the bed, getting worried by his silence. When he'd first stepped into the room, I had thought that maybe something had happened at the studio, but this was more than that.

"I gotta tell you somethin shorty, but I want you to know that I'ma handle this shit." He was talking in a calming way, like whatever he was about to tell me was going to really piss me off. All types of things ran through my mind, mostly scenarios with bitches or another hoe claiming to be having his baby.

"Okaaaaaay," I said slowly, trying to prepare myself. Judah came over to where I sat on the bed and took a seat next to me, grabbing ahold of my hands and holding them in his own, but I snatched away. "Just tell me Judah!" He seemed like he was stalling and I wanted him to just go ahead and rip the band aid off. I wasn't the same Nivea; I wasn't about to just put up with anything to keep a man around. My mind was already full of all types of terrible things that he could have done, and I was already starting the shutting down on him process.

"Girl, I know you better calm yo lil ass down! I ain't did shit!" he fumed with his ears turning red.

"I can't tell! You brought yo ass in here lookin all guilty and shit and sayin that you had to tell me somethin!"

"That's cause what I gotta tell you is fucked up, but I ain't did shit!" He side-eyed me, and I kind of felt bad for thinking the worst right away. He got off the bed and began to pace in front of me. "Nivea, I'm tryna be cool and not go fuck some shit up right now, that's how fucked up I am about this shit! I don't even know how to tell you somethin like this for real!"

Now, I was getting scared for real. The only thing that would have Judah so mad that he knew I would be upset about was my kids, and I prayed nothing involving my kids had happened. I climbed off the bed and grabbed his shoulder so that he would stop going back and forth.

"Judah, please tell me what happened!"

He took a deep breath and nodded, then led me back over to the bed, kneeling in front of me as soon as I sat down.

"Bae, Ky just told me that- that Jay touched her before... and Quad knew about it," he finally revealed. I shook my head; I just couldn't believe that! Jumping to my feet, I tried to leave out of the room, but he wrapped his arms around my waist and held me so that I couldn't get away.

"Nivea!"

"No! No Judah! Let me go! I wanna talk to my baby!" I fought him off, but he wasn't letting up.

"Nivea! Fuck man, you gotta calm down! You can't go in there actin all crazy or she ain't gone tell you shit! It's a reason why she ain't say nothin to you; she might be scared of how you gone react or if you'll believe her!" he said into my ear. As hard as it was for me to listen to him, I knew that me going in there acting a fool and screaming the way that I wanted to would probably only make her clam up. There was no telling how long she'd kept this secret from me! And to think that Quad knew the whole time, she probably thought I ain't give a fuck about what had happened to her. All this damn time I had been feeling really bad about his mama and Jay getting killed, and thinking that the reason why Kymia had such an attitude with him was because he had left. When she was angry because of him allowing her to be hurt.

Judah spun me around in his arms and embraced me as I cried, rubbing my back. I asked myself over and over again what I could have done to help? What type of mother was I that I didn't notice? It was like my kid had been crying out to me and I'd been ignoring her and focusing on some of every-thing else and Quad. She probably thought I was crazy mourning the death of Jay and his mama, when he had violated her in the worst way. I didn't know how long it took me to finally calm down but, when I finally stopped crying, Judah held my face and told me that it was going to be okay and I believed him.

"I promise shorty, I got that nigga Quad. All I want you to worry about is taking care of Ky... you got that?"

I nodded, despite not knowing if I would be able to handle things. I had to admit that the small pep talk from Judah made me feel a little better but, besides the despair that I was feeling, anger was the underlying emotion that I felt.

It felt like I was walking the green mile to Kymia's room when I finally got the nerve to go there. She was lying on her back with her headphones in, so she didn't know I was there until I came and sat down on the air mattress beside her.

"Savage told you, didn't he?" she said flatly, only turning her head in my direction. It took everything in me not to cry at how unemotional she sounded about the whole thing.

"Yeah, he told me... but why didn't you tell me?"

She huffed and then finally sat up and slammed her headphones on the bed. "Would you believe me if I did? All you ever be worried about is work, and QJ and Quiana, and Quad! Then, when he left, it just got worse, and you already seemed like you had so much on yo plate! It would have just been another thing that stressed you out and that's *if* you even believed me!" she snapped with tears in her eyes. She was unloading on me, and I didn't have any idea that she saw me that way. Completely self-absorbed and only worried about myself and her siblings and not paying attention to her.

"Yes, I would have believed you! You're my baby! I just been so busy trying to make sure that you guys had everything that you needed, I guess I didn't think nothin of the way you been acting lately, but you barely seem like you want my attention whenever I talk to you," I stuttered, trying to explain.

"Well, I did! I wanted you to ask me what was wrong! You be so worried bout everything else tho! You didn't even know this happened a long time ago! It was when you was working the night shift and we had to stay at Quad's mama house. He caught me coming out of the bathroom and pushed me back in."

"Did he... did he?" I motioned at her private area, wondering how far he had gone with my baby and horrified at the thought that he may have taken her innocence.

"No, he just touched it some. I told Quad and his mama the next day, but she said I was lyin and Quad just told me not to ever say nothin about it and he would make sure that it didn't happen no more." She'd pulled her knees up at this point and held her legs tightly. I grabbed her up into a hug and squeezed her to me.

"I swear to God if you had told me that any of them had shit to do with this, I would have killed all of their asses myself! The last thing I ever want is for you to feel like I wouldn't care if something happened to you. I love you, do you understand me!" I pulled away and looked her in the eyes, hoping that she understood how much I loved her. "Don't ever feel like you can't come to me about anything, no matter what."

She nodded, and I prayed that she meant it. It was hard for me to believe that she felt like I didn't care, even though everything that I did was for her and her siblings but, between the drama of my own life and work, I had made her feel unimportant somehow. I didn't care what I needed to do, I would make sure that she never felt that way again.

CHAPTER 22

$\mathcal{N}$iyah
I was in a bad mood. Not only had some detectives come up to my job to question me about Troy, but I got a call from my mama telling me that DCFS was there to remove the kids from her house. I hadn't told anyone that I had them, so either Kisha had made it a point to inform them of her kids' whereabouts, or they'd finally gotten ahold of Kenyon. I lied and told them that there was a family emergency so that I could leave work. Now, I was stuck in traffic and it was taking me even longer to get to them. My phone rang with yet another call from my mama, and I decided to just not answer since the line of cars had finally started to move.

I arrived at her house not even ten minutes later, but they were already gone. My mama came outside wringing her hands and crying.

"Niyah! They took them! There was nothin I could do! Kenyon was found dead this morning and they've been looking for Kisha because she was the last one to have seen him alive!"

"What! I knew that crazy bitch had did something to him!" I fumed. I knew my cousin was crazy, but I ain't think she was "murder" somebody crazy. Now, they'd come and taken her kids to some type of foster care because of her bad decisions and I was more than sure her ass ain't give a fuck about where they ended up.

"That's what they're saying, that Kisha did this. They left a card for you to call them so that they could let you know more." She was emotional as hell, crying and carrying on and I was trying to think.

"Come on, let's go inside so I can call them and find out what they're going to do with the girls." We walked into the house and I sat my things down while she ran to get the card out of the kitchen, and my phone started going off with calls from Troy. I started not to pick up because I was already dealing with some shit, but I wanted to curse his ass out anyway for me having to deal with the police at work of all places.

Hello? Niyah, you there baby?" he said as soon as he realized the phone wasn't ringing anymore.

"Yeah, I'm here. Why did the police come asking me questions about you today at work?" I frowned. My mama had returned by now and handed me the card.

"Cause I was with yo ass the other night and they needed proof of that," he said simply.

"Well, don't you think that me being questioned by the police at work wasn't a good look? Couldn't they have caught me walkin or some shit like they do on t.v.?" I was talking to him but scanning the card in my hand. The lady's name that had taken the girls was Bernice Andrews.

"I can't control when them niggas come question people, shit. They probably came to yo job to make you nervous, but don't even worry about it. They shouldn't be botherin' you again."

"They better not cause I already gotta try and get the girls back. Kisha's crazy ass killed their daddy, so me and my mama is the only family they got right now." I cried, feeling beyond stressed.

"Daaaaaamn, shorty was out here doin it like that?" He sounded completely shocked, but I wasn't. I didn't know what had happened to make Kisha turn into the nut that she was. She'd always been weird but, like I said, she was my cousin, almost like my sister. Who would have thought that she would turn out like this? Beating her kids and killing their father for no reason.

I'd completely checked out of the conversation, so I didn't know what the hell Troy was talking about anymore by the time I tuned back in to what he was saying.

"What you say?" I asked, sighing heavily.

"I asked if you wanted me to come get you from yo mama crib?" His voice was full of worry and, despite the situation, I couldn't help but gush at how much of a three sixty he'd done since we figured out our situation.

"Aww, that's sweet bae, but I gotta talk to this lady about the girls, so I'll be here for a while. If you're gonna be home later, I can just come over there."

"That's cool, I gotta go to this meeting with the people at the record label, but just hit me up and let me know when you on yo way."

"Okay, bye."

"Ayite." He always hung up without saying good-bye with his petty ass. After disconnecting the call, I dialed up the lady Bernice but only got her voicemail. I figured she was still in route to wherever it was that she was taking my cousins, so I just went ahead and left her a message, with my name, relation to the girls, and a call back number.

All I could do was hope and pray that she called me back soon and that she wouldn't be quick to put them with a family before we could talk. I didn't have any clue about whether or not I was prepared to raise not one but two children, especially considering that I felt my mama was too old to be trying to start all over. What I did know though was that I didn't want them in the system and I would do whatever it was that I needed so that they wouldn't be.

CHAPTER 23

Troy

Having taken care of Keys, a small bit of the weight was lifted off of my shoulders. Even though new problems were arising damn near every day. Not only had Quad tried to kill our asses, but he had violated Nivea's daughter by letting his bum ass brother get away with touching her. I know my nigga was fucked up having to deal with shit like that cause I was even having a hard time dealing with the news, and I wasn't even directly involved. In addition to all of that, Niyah was trying to get custody of her cousins because Kisha had gone crazy and killed their father. I had been in the system my whole life, so I understood her reasoning for not wanting them to have to go through that, but I wasn't sure at my age if I was ready to be serious with a female with kids. Shit, I'd barely wanted to be serious with her from the beginning and now she was adding kids to the mix. I wasn't Savage. I wasn't built to be jumping straight into the family life, especially when I'd never really had one of my own to learn from.

"So, where you meet this bitch at again?" I asked Savage as we sat in the studio smoking.

"Shit, she came at me when I was leavin here the other day." He shrugged and took a pull of the blunt, holding the smoke in his mouth before releasing it into the air and passing it to me. I couldn't help raising an eyebrow at that piece of information.

"Soooo, his side bitch came up here for you to set that nigga up?" I couldn't lie, that shit was suspect as hell to me. I hadn't ever seen no bitch ready to turn on her nigga like that.

"Yeah, I know, right. She said that nigga been on some other shit, puttin his hands on her and sayin he gone kill her ass if she have his baby. But, get this shit though, her ass met him workin at the prison he was in-"

"Wait! This bitch in law enforcement?" I had to be sure I was hearing his ass right. There wasn't no fucking way that Savage was willing to trust anything this hoe was talking about; he couldn't be that dumb. His ass had to be desperate as hell!

"Nigga, she fuckin security at a prison! Her ass ain't no police, and she old as shit with a whole husband and kid already! You know how them hoes be when they work around a bunch of niggas in jail. They be horny as fuck! Bitch already risked it all even messin with that nigga." Of course what he was saying was true. We'd heard plenty of niggas talking about how they had a female CO under their thumb while they were locked down. And all their asses ended up right back in the box once the bitch realized that they were only together behind bars.

"Mannnn, I don't know. You don't think this bitch might be settin you up?" He let out a slick grin then and snatched the blunt out my hand.

"She can't set me up nigga! You think I'm stupid enough to trust shit that come out her mouth. Hell naw! I followed her dumb ass home. She told me she got an apartment with Quad's ass." He looked at me, still grinning with his eyebrows raised up like I understood what the fuck he was getting at.

"Okaaaay and?"

"And she never gave me her address, all she told me was to call her and she would help me set him up." He paused, waiting for me to catch on, but I must have been high as fuck because I still didn't know. "Boy, lay off the weed! If she never told me her address, then she can't say that I knew where to find Quad."

I nodded slowly, finally getting what he was saying. Even if she told us anything about Quad without admitting where we could find him, there was no way that they could pin his murder on us, even if she did talk.

"Ohhh okay, so when we sposed to go over there?"

"Right now," he said, quickly sitting up in his chair.

"Like right, right now?"

"Yeah, we already signed into the studio, and I know a way that we can leave out and come back in without anybody seein us."

"Bet," I agreed. I was more than ready to get this shit over with. It would be one less thing to worry about and give me more time to focus on the music and how I was going to handle things with Niyah.

Twenty minutes later, we were leaving out of one of the backdoors in the studio. Savage stuck some tape on the latch to make sure that we could get back in the same way and we were gone without anybody knowing. He said it was better for us to leave our phones back at the studio so that if they tracked them, it wouldn't show us hitting the cell towers near Quad's body or his house.

"So, you sure that nigga gone come?" I asked, looking over at Savage in the passenger seat. The plan was to wait until he got to the house and just go in and get him, but we would have to kill shorty if she was there too. We wasn't leaving no witnesses and she could definitely vouch that it was two niggas that came in her crib after she had talked to Savage. Nah, we wanted to catch him coming or going.

"Yeah, she basically said that he sleep here every night, she just don't," he told me with his eyes glued to the apartment that was across the street.

"Mannnnn, we gone have to kill this bitch watch." He finally turned my way with a scowl. I could understand him not wanting to kill somebody else that ain't have shit to do with this, but I just couldn't trust this whole thing. It seemed way too easy for us, even though she hadn't given him the address.

"Nigga, she ain't even here."

"How you know? She could be up there waitin on him or yo ass right now!" I was all about tying up this loose end, but not if it just caused more trouble for us.

"Because her car gone, all the lights out and it's night time. It ain't even no t.v. light on, how many bitches you know gone sit in a dark house by they self?" He ticked off each reason on his fingers and gave me a pointed look in the dark.

"Ayite, so what if she with him when he pull up?"

"She not gone be with him cause she said the last time she was here, he beat her ass and made her miscarry. She was leavin the hospital when she stopped at the studio. And I saw her paperwork, she had a miscarriage. Trust me nigga, I thought this whole shit out." Now that shit had me believing him. Quad should have known better than to fuck with a bitch's baby. Probably the second that baby died, so did her feelings for that nigga.

"Aye, there go her car right there." He pointed as a silver Focus pulled up in front of the building and turned the lights out. Without waiting on me to say or do anything, Savage hopped out of the car, closing the door quietly behind him at the same time that Quad exited his own vehicle. I leaned forward in the seat and watched as Savage eased across the street and came up behind him with his gun drawn, instantly stopping him in his tracks. Savage didn't waste any time sending two bullets through the back of that nigga's skull, neither of which alerted anybody because of the silencer he had attached to his gun.

I waited, thinking that he would come right back, but was surprised to see him bend down and take something out of that nigga's hand. I realized it was the car keys when he went around and popped the trunk.

"What the fuck is this nigga doin?" I mumbled to myself as I watched him run back to Quad and drag him back to the trunk, tossing him inside and closing it back before motioning for my attention. Confused, I pulled over to where he stood in the street and rolled down the passenger side window.

"Nigga, what the fuck is you doin?" I asked as soon as he stuck his head in the window.

"Just follow me right quick, you'll see." He was out of breath and I ain't know if it was from excitement or from lifting that big ass nigga up. Just as fast as he'd come over, he was gone sliding into the driver's side of Quad's car and driving off. I followed closely behind him all the way to the fucking water front. We drove down until we reached a secluded area where there wasn't anybody around and I parked and got out once I saw him exit the car.

"Ayite, so what the fuck you got planned?" I finally asked, meeting him at the car door. He grinned widely like his ass had the secret recipe to krabby patties.

"Okay, so you know that we're gonna be the first niggas that the police come lookin for as soon as his body is discovered right. So, I figured that if I shoot him outside of the building he lives in with Desiree, and then put him in her car..."

"She'll be the one that they hit up for killin him," I finished off his sentence with a smile and nod of my own.

"Exactly! Plus, it's paperwork provin that she had a miscarriage because he beat her ass," he added. Now, I was getting what he was saying. If the body was found, they might come question us, but the evidence would all point to his bitch.

"My muthafuckin nigga!"

"Right, now help me push this shit in so we can go." I ran around to the passenger side while he stayed where he was, putting the car in neutral. After the car was completely submerged in the lake, we stood outside taking off the joggers and hoodies we wore, leaving only wife beaters and basketball shorts. I put everything, including our shoes into a garbage bag, tied it up and threw it into the trunk.

"You a smart ass lil nigga, you know that?" I laughed, getting in and speeding off.

"I been knew, catch up, my dude."

We ended up dumping the bag inside of one of the dumpsters behind a McDonald's on the way back to the studio and changed into some different hoodies and jeans before we snuck back in. That shit hadn't taken no more than a couple hours and we were already back recording our song like ain't shit even happen.

CHAPTER 24

*N*ivea

"Today, a correctional officer named Desiree Engle was arrested in connection to the death of Quad Mitchell. A month ago, Mitchell went missing and his body was discovered in the trunk of Engle's car earlier this week after it was pulled out of Lake Michigan. Engle is being charged with first degree murder and obstruction of justice. We'll keep you posted on this story as we gather information."

"How many times you gone watch them talk about this shit?" Judah said, cutting the t.v. off and throwing the remote back down beside me on our king size bed.

"As many times as I want to, that muthafucka deserved worse." I was still a little mad that I didn't get to experience Quad's death, so watching any news about it always helped some. Since word had gotten back about him going missing, the police automatically came around questioning me, Judah, Troy and Niyah, but all of our alibis had checked out. They were more than pissed that they didn't have any way to prove Judah's involvement and, without either of their star witnesses, his lawyer immediately moved for all charges to be dropped against him for Jay and his mama's murder.

"Yo lil violent ass," he chuckled, climbing into bed with me. "Who woulda thought sweet ole Nivea was a Savage?"

"Oh, you got jokes huh? You lucky I like yo ass." I playfully punched him in the stomach and he wrestled me down, pinning my arms on either side of my head as he rested between my thighs.

"You only like me, huh?" he questioned, leaning down and biting my neck enough to make me yelp in a mixture of pain and pleasure. It felt good not having to worry about Quad or Kisha's crazy asses. And it felt even better having my man in the physical and not behind bars. Judah had proposed to me a couple of weeks before and, while I was happy, I decided to have a long engagement so that we had more time together before we jumped into something he wasn't ready for, but he showed me every day how much he loved me and the kids.

Speaking of the kids, none of them seemed too torn up about Quad being dead, not even Quiana. I guess seeing him the way he was after he'd left prison had turned them all against him, if his absence hadn't already done so. Kymia was doing much better. We'd gotten her a psychiatrist and she had been making good strides in opening up about her feelings and behaving better at home and in school. I know she had a long way to go yet, but I was proud of the things she'd accomplished since telling me about what Jay had done.

Niyah was still working overtime to get her cousins out of the foster home that they were in. Since they came from such a terrible background, the courts were worried about releasing them to Niyah, but she was passing every test that they put in front of her and she was hoping to have them living with her in the next six months. And her and Troy were going stronger than ever. Surprisingly, he had even taken a parenting course since he knew that he would be around the girls also. I guess he wasn't so bad after all.

"I said what I said." I tried to be stubborn and wiggle away.

"Ayite, then let me just go sleep with QJ." He shrugged while moving away, but I wrapped my arms around his neck and held him in place.

"Okay, okay. You know I love yo savage ass." I smirked, leaning up to kiss those pink ass lips I loved so much.

"That's what you better had said." He covered my body with his again and I relished in the feeling. Nothing had ever felt better than being with Judah. Who would have thought I would let a cold ass Savage steal my heart?

The End...

Made in the USA
Middletown, DE
18 July 2021